Matt Dillon eased out his Colt's and took a step forward. Pilcher, reaching for the latch to swing the door closed, caught Matt's movement in the darkness. He straightened and reached for his own gun.

"Hold it!" Matt said.

Pilcher froze. He peered at the figure before the door, still partly in the dark. Matt took another step and stood full in the beam of light from the doorway. He let Pilcher get a good look at the gun he was holding.

"Well, Marshal, I *wanted* to see you again before I left," Pilcher said.

"Daggett told me that," Matt said.

"That murderin' sidewinder!" Pilcher's voice rose. "He killed the best friend I ever had!"

Matt saw that Pilcher was working himself up to the point where he might make a desperate try for his gun. "Don't make a fool play!" he warned.

Pilcher's hand flashed to his gun and up. He was fast, terribly fast. . . .

—One brief, pungent scene from the scores in this adaptation of CBS' great TV show:

G U N S M O K E

Don Ward

10 Short Stories Based on the CBS TV Program

GUNSMOKE

Ballantine Books • New York

Library of Congress Catalog Card No. 57-14674

BALLANTINE BOOKS, INC.
101 Fifth Avenue, New York 3, N. Y.

Contents

INTRODUCTION

"The Wickedest Little City in America"

Whether Dodge City actually rated that appellation or not, it very probably was the most colorfully uproarious of all the famous frontier towns. The little community on the north bank of the Arkansas River, situated on the Old Santa Fe Trail, saw its share or more of bullwhackers and muleskinners. Five miles from Fort Dodge, it provided a place for soldiers on pass to spend their pay and have themselves a time. As "Buffalo City," it was the capital of the hide hunters who worked the plenty-buffalo area where the grazing grounds of the great Arkansas and Texas herds overlapped. The hide hunters liked their fun on the rough side, too, and they found it in the town that was renamed Dodge City, after the near-by fort, when the railroad came in, in 1872.

It was in that year that the first big herd of longhorns—two thousand head—was driven to Dodge. There were as yet no loading pens, so that herd kept going until it got to Great Bend. 1875 was the first year to see cattle shipped regularly from Dodge; from then until 1885 Dodge City was, veritably, the Cowboy Capital. In that period, this town of about one thousand permanent inhabitants saw its population swell during the April-September shipping season every year with the addition of one to two thousand cowboys, many of whom hung around for several weeks, getting rid of six months', or even perhaps a year's, pay.

They had no trouble getting rid of it. They spent some of it on clothing and equipment; the saloonkeepers, the gamblers, and the girls were ready, willing and able to relieve them of the rest. After a fall and winter in Texas, and then months on the trail, during which they might average sixteen

7

or more hours in the saddle daily, they were bent on excitement. They got it. Sometimes they created it, by their own riotous behavior. "It was their dream," Stanley Vestal has said, "to hurrah the town, to kill the Marshal or run him out of town, to 'tree' the camp, and then, with DODGE painted on the canvas cover of their chuckwagon, to ride home to Texas and declare, 'We taken Dodge.' "

Well, there had to be someone to handle such young men as these, problem children the like of which America will never see again. To do this job, a succession of peace officers served Dodge City whose names include the illustrious ones of Bat Masterson and his brothers, Wyatt Earp, and Bill Tilghman; and lesser known ones like Billy Rivers, Jack Allen, Luke Short, and Neal Brown. Taken together, they made up a formidable company. In spite of all the lore, though, the number of killings recorded by these Dodge City lawmen was not high. Earp and Bat Masterson, for example, hung up only one each during their terms of service. They were more likely to disarm and arrest a man, or subdue him with a pistol-whipping, or, often, establish order out of turbulence by the sheer force of their arrival and presence on the scene. They were ready to sling lead if they had to. Generally, they didn't have to.

Of such man-stuff, largely, is television's Marshal Matt Dillon. More on the thoughtful side, maybe. More concerned with the why's of men's actions, more aware of the limitations that beset human beings. More keenly alive to moral as well as legal responsibilities, perhaps.

And perhaps that is why he is so popular.

REUNION '78

Dodge City's Long Branch saloon was enjoying an unaccustomed quiet night. The bar was lightly patronized and the two aprons moved back and forth behind it with a leisurely air, setting out a bottle, taking a coin, making desultory talk. The gaming tables in the rear were getting a fair play but the customers there were being surprisingly unvocal.

Seated at a table with Kitty Russell, Marshal Matt Dillon noted the relative silence prevailing in this normally tumultuous place and remarked on it to his pretty table companion.

"Kind of unusual for the Long Branch." He made wet circles on the table top with the bottom of his half-empty glass. "Unusual for Dodge City, come to that," he added.

"Thank heaven a time like this does come along once in a while," Kitty responded. "Believe me, Matt, we can use an easy hour when we get it. Both of us."

Matt smiled. "My work comes in fits and starts," he told her. "But you're going it hot and heavy most of the time. In fact, the reason I came in," he confided, "was to get you to sit down for a minute—didn't know then what a soft touch you were having tonight."

She gave him a mock salute. "Good Samaritan Dillon," she said, quirking her lips at him. "I don't know if I can stand you so saintly."

"Won't have to, long," He made some more circles. "Got to finish the street, get back to the office for a while."

Her eyes held his face for a moment. "Make it in again later," she said. "I might need you to slow me down then; I don't think this will last."

He sighed. "You're right. There's two trail outfits still camped a ways out. They'll be showing, sooner or later, and then there'll be no rest for the wicked."

"Meaning me, I suppose?" She tilted her head, eyebrows arched.

"Meaning all of us." Matt Dillon said it lightly, but his lips showed no smile. "Show me a man and I'll show you a sinner. We all tote a share of it—some of us more than others, that's all."

Kitty Russell looked at this lawman, her eyes warm and gentle. "I know how you feel, Matt. You—bear a heavier load than most of us, maybe because you let your conscience take on what a lot of other people shoulder aside . . . Oh, Matt, why don't you get away from this town?" she burst out.

"A lot of good people in Dodge City," he reminded her. "Not angels, maybe—but good people. I work for them. My job is to make this place tolerable. Later on, it'll be somebody's else's job to keep it a proud place to live. You know how I feel, Kitty . . . there are worse places than Dodge City."

"It's a better place because you're here, Matt," she said quietly. She looked up as a middle-aged, erect man approached their table. "Well, Pete, I didn't expect to see you back here so soon? Where's Belle?"

Captain Peter Wynn, breveted Lieutenant Colonel in the Civil War, was a retired U. S. Army officer with a little money who had been living in Dodge for several months, and spending a large part of his time hanging around the Long Branch. It was no secret that the place's attraction for him lay in the charms of Belle Archer, one of its prettiest girls.

"Outside," Pete Wynn answered briefly. He picked up the woman's garment draped over the back of the vacant chair at the table. "She asked me to get her cape and take her home."

Kitty frowned and started to rise. "Is there something wrong, Pete? Anything I can do to help?"

"No, thanks, Kitty," Wynn said. "She just said to tell you she's going to her room, that she doesn't feel so well." He looked uncertain. "Headache, I guess."

"That's tough," Kitty said. "Tell her not to worry about us, Pete. Have her take an aspirin and go to bed and get a good sleep for a change. Wait, I'll tell her myself."

Wynn nodded briefly to Matt and headed for the door, Kitty hurrying along with him.

Matt raised one finger to Wynn in a vague farewell gesture. He was engrossed in watching two men at the bar.

One of them was wearing "store" clothes. His appearance

was that of a town man, but Matt, who had talked to him a couple of times, felt that the designation somehow didn't quite fit the fellow. His name was Andy Culley and he was a hardware and farm-equipment salesman. He had recently added a new item—something he called barbed wire—to his line, and he was tiresomely voluble about it. Matt had been subjected to a rapid-fire talk on the new product's virtues earlier in the day and he suspected that the bartender, who had been serving Culley with a blank face and half-raised eyebrows, was being treated to the same dose.

A few minutes earlier a newcomer had sided Culley at the bar. He was in his middle or late twenties, Matt judged, lean and tanned, his face an interesting combination of strength and sensitivity. He wore the garb of a trail driver, and Matt, who had never seen the man before, assumed he was a rider for one of the two outfits that had just crossed the Arkansas with their herds and were waiting to get their stuff into the shipping pens.

The trail driver was obviously alone, but upon coming in he had unhesitatingly taken a position at the bar right next to Culley, ignoring the empty spaces extending on each side of the salesman. He had ordered a whisky and stood there, ignoring it after one quick sip, shooting glances at Culley, listening to his gab, seeming to size the man up.

As Matt observed the tableau, Culley appeared to be getting ready to pay his tab and leave. He wiped his mouth, straightened the hat on his head, spoke to Mike, the bartender, and reached into his pants pocket. The good-looking young trailsman interposed, throwing a coin on the bar, waving a hand at Mike, and looking expectantly and—Matt thought—challengingly at Culley. Culley said something and grinned at the younger man, but there was a tension about his face that made Matt Dillon, who had an eye for such things, sit straight in his chair, and bring all his attention on the two.

Kitty, who had followed Pete Wynn out to have her word with Belle, slipped back into her seat.

"She's a strange one," Kitty remarked.

"What's that?" Matt said, not turning his head.

"Belle Archer, I mean." Kitty lifted her drink and sipped it. "Not coming back. Headache, my eye. She acts like she's plain scared, to me. Of what, I don't know."

"Yeah?" Matt said, still looking toward the two at the bar.

"I can't help wondering about her," Kitty said. "Where she came from . . . what brought her here. She never talks about herself . . . she's kind of a puzzle to me."

Matt said, "I got another one for you—why's the cowboy picking the fight with the hardware drummer?"

Kitty's attention went to the scene at the bar. Culley, red-faced and sweating, was half-turned toward the door, as though anxious to get away. The trailsman was in the act of pouring another drink into the glass that Culley had already emptied, quickly once, at the other's insistence. The bartender was watching them worriedly.

Matt got to his feet and moved unobtrusively toward them. He got close enough to hear Culley say: "Sorry, mister, I've got to get back to the hotel."

He started away but the cowboy grabbed his arm. "Let's not get insulting, now," he said harshly.

The bartender leaned forward. "The man says no, he means no," he told the trailsman. He reached to pick up the bottle that sat on the bar.

The rider quickly put his own hand on it. "Leave it there." He pushed the shotglass full of whisky at Culley. "Drink it."

Culley looked at it, looked at the other's set face, looked away. "I said I'm going," he announced weakly.

"And I said drink it," the cowboy persisted. "Better bring another bottle, bartender. Andy here's goin' to drink to the old home town till he drops."

With a sudden movement of his left arm Culley knocked the shotglass out of the trail man's proffering hand and then swept the bottle off the bar top. Glass and bottle crashed on the floor. Men rose quickly from tables, faced about at the bar, staring.

With a muttered oath, the trail driver grabbed Culley's left arm, twisted it in a hammerlock, spun the man around and pinned him against the bar.

The drummer was sweating profusely now; from his pain-twisted mouth came a whining "Let go, let go!"

Matt Dillon stepped forward to break it up, then paused as the tense-faced young man, holding Culley tight with the hammerlock grip, shoved the drummer's right sleeve up to the elbow. Matt peered forward as the trailsman bent over the exposed forearm. On the man's pale skin he saw tattooed a letter Q boxed by a diamond.

The rider's voice was harsh and strained: "I was right." Loosing his grip on the other's left arm he yanked him around. Culley's face was a study in fear. The trail man balled his fists. "I ought to kill you," he grunted. He punched the drummer in the face. Culley sagged and the other hit him again, a swinging smash to the jaw. Culley staggered back against the bar. The rider crowded after him and landed another punch to the drummer's face. Culley fell sidewise to the floor and lay still.

The whole sequence of violent action had taken no more than ten or twelve seconds. Once it started, Matt Dillon had no chance to stop it. He'd been momentarily thrown off by the exposure of the tattoo mark on the drummer's arm. Now he had to act. He stepped toward the trail driver again, being careful to stay more than arm's length from him. It was always a mistake to get too close to a man who was quick with his fists.

Mike, the bartender, was leaning over to take a look at the half-conscious Culley. "Holy smoke," he muttered, and looked up at the defiant trail driver. Kitty's voice came to Matt above the murmuring of the other onlookers: "Get him out of here!" she was saying.

The trailsman had swung to face the spectators crowding about. "Stay back," he warned. "I'm not finished with him." His hand hovered over his holstered gun.

"Yes, you are." Matt's voice brought the other's head around to look at the lawman. "You're finished here, friend."

"Keep out of this, Marshal," the trailsman said in a level voice. "I said I'm not finished with him. I got a ways to go yet."

"That you do," Matt said. "About two hundred feet. From here to the jail."

The trailsman's hand moved almost imperceptibly nearer the butt of his holstered gun. Matt stood still, ready himself, not wanting to use his gun if he could help it, watching the other's eyes, keeping his own face calm, thinking that this shouldn't have been allowed to develop, that he should have moved in sooner, when he first saw the conflict brewing in the tension, in the attitudes of this man and the drummer, pleading silently that the other's gun hand be stayed.

"Don't do it," he said quietly.

Culley made a diversion by stirring, shaking his head, groping uncertainly to his feet. The trailsman turned his head slightly to glance at the man he had attacked. Then he looked back at Matt and let his right hand drop quietly to his side.

Matt Dillon sighed inwardly and let himself relax. "Come on, mister," he said. "Let's go." He headed the trailsman toward the door. First warning the other that he was going to do so, he pulled the man's gun from its holster and walked along behind him, holding the weapon in his left hand.

Someone was saying in a hushed voice, "Can you beat that?" and another man asked querulously, "Who the devil started it, anyhow? Does anybody know?"

Matt took a backward glimpse as he followed his prisoner out the door. Mike, the bartender, was looking concernedly at Culley, his lips moving in some kind of comment or question, as the drummer lifted a glass of whisky to his lips, a little unsteadily.

In the marshal's office, Matt tossed the prisoner's gun on his desk, had the man shuck his cartridge belt and add it to the pile. Matt sat down behind the desk and pulled out a report blank.

"What's your name?"

"Jerry Shand."

"Well, sit down over there. . . . They must grow 'em real tough where you come from, Shand. Roughing up a hardware drummer with a pot belly. Real two-fisted, he-man stuff."

"You're a real talky kind of marshal, too," Shand said sourly.

"Well, I've got more patience than some. Maybe you might give a little thought to the advantages of getting talked at instead of pistol-whipped. You've been around long enough to know what sort of treatment you'd be getting from some lawmen."

"Yeah, I'm real grateful," the other said, but Matt thought he detected a note of genuine contrition under the sarcastic words.

"What's your outfit?" he said shortly.

"Lazy K," was the response. "From the Pecos."

Matt scribbled. "When'd you pull in?"

"This afternoon."

"Where's the rest of your crew?"

"Out at the holdin' ground. Couple of us got leave to come in ahead of the rest."

"A couple? Where's your partner?"

"Lost him outside. He's not much of a drinkin' man. Lookin' for faster action down the street somewheres."

"What call did you have to pick on Andy Culley, there in the Long Branch? Got something against him?"

Shand did not reply.

"You don't even know him, do you? Just hit town at the end of the trail, feeling ringy, and look for a fight? Why didn't you choose somebody who could give you a run for your money?"

"Listen, Marshal," Shand said tightly, "you don't know what this is all about."

Matt looked at him. "All right; you tell me, then."

"It's—personal between him and me," Shand said stubbornly.

"Well," Matt said evenly, "have you got twenty-five dollars bail money to put up?"

"No, I haven't. Boss pays off tomorrow."

"Then you can spend a peaceful night here on a jailhouse bunk. I wish it would teach you and your Texas saddlemates to keep your hands folded when you get north of the Deadline—but I don't reckon it will," Matt ended with a sigh.

He and Shand looked around as the door opened. It was Andy Culley. He had a cut lip and a mouse under one eye. He glanced once at Shand, who was staring malevolently at him, and then turned his gaze to Matt.

"Evening, Marshal," said the drummer.

"What is it, Culley?"

"I—don't want to butt in, Marshal," Culley said hesitantly, taking a couple of slow steps toward the desk.

"You already have," Matt said drily; "but go ahead— what's on your mind?"

Culley licked his lips and flicked a glance at Shand, who had risen quickly from his chair. "I, uh, just wanted to tell him—I'm sorry . . ." the drummer said.

Matt stared at him. "*You're* sorry?"

"Yeah—for starting the fracas over there. I maybe said something I shouldn't."

There was a silence. The marshal and his prisoner thought about this strange statement, each in his own way, trying to fit it into the framework of his own knowledge. It was Culley who broke the silence.

"You aren't bringing assault charges against him, Marshal —because I won't sign a complaint."

"You don't need to," Matt said shortly. "I was there and I saw what happened. Shand here picked a fight."

"Well, I won't have no part in it," Culley said; "I don't want no trouble."

"Disturbing the peace happens to be a misdemeanor— even in Dodge City." Matt wondered where this was all leading to.

"Well, then, what's the bail?" Culley demanded.

"Twenty-five dollars," Matt said wearily.

Culley thrust a hand into his trousers pocket and brought it out filled with gold coins. He counted out five and dropped them on Matt's desk. "There you are." He looked at Jerry Shand. "It's the least I can do, boy," he said to the trailsman, and went out.

Matt was watching Jerry Shand. The young rider's face was bleak, his mouth a grim, uncompromising line, as he kept his eyes on the retreating drummer's back.

The marshal pushed his hat back with an exasperated grunt. He did not offer a word as Jerry Shand lifted his gun and rig from the desk and buckled the belt around his middle. Shand's eyes were blank, his expression cold and noncommittal, as he met Matt's stare. He turned, strode to the door, and went out into the night.

Slowly, Matt Dillon tore the partially filled-out blank from the pad in front of him. Eyes troubled, he crumpled it in a wad, ending with a vicious twist, and threw it into a corner.

There was something wrong here, something that had its roots in the past. A past that the drummer wanted to forget . . . that young Shand wouldn't forget, and wasn't going to let Culley forget. . . .

Matt remembered the tattooing on Culley's arm. A Q in a diamond. It identified Culley as a former follower of William Clark Quantrill, colonel in the Confederate Army and notorious guerrilla chieftain in the no-quarter border fighting in Missouri and Kansas. Any man who had fought with Quantrill's raiders was sure to have made enemies—lasting ones. Jerry Shand looked too young to have been involved in the border fighting, though; this was 1878, thirteen years after the end of hostilities. Shand must be carrying on some kind of blood feud that dated back to the war years. . . .

Matt Dillon thought somberly of the bitter differences that all too often still set one American against another. The War was long over, and bygones, no matter how vividly experienced and recalled, should be no more than bygones. But the scars that had been inflicted were long-lasting and slow to heal, and occasionally something like this came along, a result of the fanaticism of a John Brown or the brutality of a Quantrill, an open, running sore. Making an Andy Culley cringe and crawl. Making a Jerry Shand strike out, eager to hurt and maim. Corrupting both, making them more animals than men. . . .

War was hell, yes. And for some men the aftermath of war was a special kind of hell.

Half an hour later Matt Dillon was patrolling Front Street, getting a line on the crowds that were now beginning to collect in this place and that, spotting a couple of potential troublemakers, making mental notes to look over the dodgers in his desk to check them against this or that seen face, seeing a swarthy man with his gun rigged for a cross-draw and guessing that he was maybe more proficient with the knife tucked in the back of one boot. He had just turned toward his office, meaning to spend a few minutes with those dodgers, when he heard the shot.

It came from the west end of Front Street. Looking that way, Matt saw a horse rearing, a man snatching at the bridle reins, running after the animal as it shied away. A huddled shape lay on the boardwalk near by. Drawing his gun, Matt ran toward them. As he passed the Long Branch, a crowd began pouring out through its swinging doors. Most of them legged it right after him, a few shouting hoarsely.

Matt was no more than fifteen yards away when the man caught the plunging horse. It was Jerry Shand. Matt shouted at him to halt. If the trailsman heard the command he ignored it, trying to mount, but he could not hold the shying horse still long enough to be able to toe the stirrup.

Matt stopped ten feet away from him. "Hold it, Shand," he said sharply. "My gun's on you."

Shand ceased his efforts to mount and faced the marshal, but kept his hold on the restive horse's reins. Men crowded around. Matt took Shand's gun, the cowboy offering no resistance. Pete Wynn came up. Matt handed Shand's gun to Pete and told him to keep Shand covered. Then he went over and knelt by the huddled body on the boardwalk. It was Andy Culley. He made a swift examination and rose. He glanced at Jerry Shand. The cowboy looked at him wordlessly, his face frozen.

"Somebody go get Doc Adams," Matt said. "It's a coroner case."

Several men went close enough to see that the dead man was Culley. They turned on Shand.

"Culley wasn't heeled!" one of them snarled. "Let's get this bird!"

"Yeh, string 'im up!" someone else said shrilly. The phrase was chorused by several others, over the crowd's angry muttering.

Shand was sweating and pale. "Now listen," he pleaded. "Wait a minute . . ."

"Shut up!" a redbearded man shouted at him. "Come on, boys!"

Matt drew his gun quickly. He held it waist-high. His eyes were cold. He did not raise his voice but his words lashed at them.

"That's enough of that! This is my party, boys. Nobody's going to get riled up without reason."

"Come on, Matt," a man objected huskily, "this skunk shot Culley down in cold blood!"

"If he did he'll hang for it," Matt said. "After he has a trial."

"Trial nothin'!" Redbeard shouted. "There's a limit, Matt!"

Angry yells backed him up. The crowd began to press in. Matt thumbed back the hammer of his gun. It made a startlingly loud click. Jerry Shand stood by, his face white, drawn up to his full height, his eyes on Matt.

"Stay back!" Matt whipped at them. "I mean it."

The ones in the van stopped, hesitated. Matt grasped the moment's opportunity. "Now scatter," he said quickly. "Go about your business." He paused; then: *"Fast!"*

There were a few muffled curses, but the crowd started to disperse. Matt watched them go. He let out a long breath and looked at Shand. His mouth twitching, the cowboy wiped the beads of perspiration from his forehead.

After Doc Adams had come, examined Culley and pronounced him dead, and ordered the corpse carried to the tiny county morgue, Matt made his way to his office. Shand was there, manacled and under guard, not yet in a cell. Matt sent Pete Wynn, who had brought Shand to the jail, away. He proceeded to question Shand.

"You don't have to talk if you don't want to," he said in preliminary, "but I hope you will. I'd like some answers."

"I'll talk," Shand said huskily.

"Why'd you shoot him?"

"He drew a gun on me and threatened to shoot me, that's why. I pulled my own gun and got in the first shot."

Matt looked at him. "He had a gun? We didn't find any gun on him, or around anywhere."

"He had a gun," Shand insisted. "It was a silver-mounted derringer. I got a good look at it."

"Where did it go to?"

"I don't know, darn it. Any one of that crowd could've picked it up and carried it away. All I know's he pulled it on me and I beat him to the shot."

"Well, why'd he draw on you? Why'd he want to kill you?"

"I told you, Marshal," Shand said. "It's personal."

"I think I know anyhow," Matt told him. "He was a Quantrill man—wasn't he?"

Shand looked at him for a long minute without speaking. Then he opened his mouth and the words came fast. "He was with Quantrill when they hit Lawrence in 'Sixty-three. His name isn't Culley—it's Bloody Bill Ashley—or that's what he was called then. I was just a kid but I remember it like it was yesterday. Ma made me get up and hide in the woodshed. I saw him kill my father in cold blood, and I saw that Quantrill tattoo on his arm. I—saw him drag off Ma. . . . When they rode away there wasn't anything left but smoking ruins of buildings, and dead bodies. Men and women and children. . . ."

Matt was silent as he looked at Shand. He knew the man was telling the truth. He felt a stab of compassion. But he had to go on questioning Shand, had to get the whole story if he could.

"What happened on the street?" he asked. "I thought Culley was trying to keep clear of you."

"After I left here, I got my horse," Shand said. "I was heading out of town, goin' west. Culley popped out from beside a building all of a sudden and flagged me down. I asked him what he wanted, and he said he wanted to talk to me a minute. I lit and walked over to him. I thought I'd worked off most of my hate back there in the saloon but I was about ready to slug him again.

"Then he begun to say how sorry he was, how he'd be sorry all his life, that everybody was crazy back in the war, sort of out of their heads. Wanted to make things right with me, he said, wanted to pay me.

"I said, 'Buy it back, huh? Think you can wash it all away with money?' He said what else could he do, and I said he could at least get out of Kansas. He said he couldn't do that, and then he offered me five hundred dollars. I said he must be getting rich off of Kansas now, and he said he'd make it six hundred, but he couldn't leave Kansas, he'd been in business here nearly ten years.

"I told him not many Kansans would buy his stinkin' barb' wire if they knew they was doing business with a bush-whacker. Right then he pulled that derringer and told me to shut up, and he said, 'We'll see who's through in Kansas.' Well, while he was talkin' I drew my gun—I was standing a little sideways to him and I guess maybe he didn't see what I was doing. But he was going to pull that trigger, all right. I just beat him to it. That's the God's truth, Marshal."

"Jerry," Matt said softly, "are you sure he pulled a gun?"

"Yeah, he pulled a gun." Jerry Shand put his elbows on the desk, covered his eyes with his manacled hands, and let his head sag wearily. "He pulled a gun all right," he repeated in a dull voice.

Matt Dillon was prowling around the corner where the shooting had occurred, searching in the shadows, peering down between the cracks of the boardwalk. He got down on his knees in the dust of the street to look beneath the planks of the walk. He thought he saw something glimmer but when he reached in he found only an empty tin can.

He stood up, brushing his hands together, just as Kitty Russell came up behind him.

"Matt," she said in a worried voice, "there's a bunch in the Long Branch still talking up a lynching."

"Shand claims Culley had a gun. Could be one of the lynch-law boys has it in his pocket."

"Why'd he do it, Matt? Shand, I mean."

"He seems to have had reasons. That wouldn't make any difference to the law, though. But he insists Culley had a gun and drew on him first. That'd make a difference—but no gun has showed up, and he made some threats after that fight in the bar. That'll count against him."

Kitty was looking past Matt's shoulder, up at a lighted window in the second story of a good-sized building fronting on the street.

"Looks like the only thing that could save him would be a witness, but—" Matt broke off to follow Kitty's glance. As he did so, a woman's figure appeared in the window, reaching to close the lace curtains. "That's Belle Archer, isn't it?" he asked Kitty.

"Yes—this is where she rooms."

"And she left the Long Branch early tonight, before all this happened . . . if she's been there right along . . ." He moved quickly to the base of the building and called up, "Belle!"

The woman in the window took her hand away from the curtains, leaving them partly opened, but she took a half step back into the room. She did not answer immediately.

"Belle," Matt called again, "are you up there?"

Her voice came down in faint answer: "What do you want?"

"How long have you been up there?"

Again Belle Archer did not reply, and Kitty called to her. "It's important, Belle!"

"Not—long," It sounded hesitant, uncertain.

"You see what happened down here?" Matt demanded.

There was a pause before a half-strangled "No" and a sound of sobbing came down to them. Matt and Kitty exchanged glances. "She must have seen it," he said. "She got here in plenty of time to see it all—and something's got her upset. . . . Kitty, we're going up there and talk to her."

Doc Adams, the coroner of Ford County, was presiding at the inquest held the morning after the shooting. The scene was the lobby of the Dodge House. Adams sat at a table below the balcony. To one side was the witness chair, to the other sat the half dozen members of the coroner's jury. Jerry Shand, under guard, was next to the witness chair and Kitty sat near by. A lank man with sad eyes was testifying.

"Let's proceed," Adams was saying. "You were sitting outside the Long Branch at nine last night when the accused rode up. That right?"

"That's right, Doc."

"You sure it was this Jerry Shand, right here?"

The witness pointed at Shand. "It was him, all right."

"Did you see or hear anything this court should know?"

"Y'bet I did! Somebody this feller knew was waitin' fer him. 'Is he in there?' he says, I mean Shand, and the other feller says 'Yes,' and then he says, 'Whatcha gonna do to him, Jerry?' an' this feller here says, 'I dunno, kill him, mebbe.' I recall them exact words, Doc."

"Pretty incriminatin'," Adams commented sonorously. "Remember you're under oath, Charley."

"Ed Mabry'll back me up on it!" the witness retorted with spirit. "He was right there with me, heard every dang' word!"

Jerry Shand jumped to his feet. He was trembling. "I said it, all right—but I didn't mean it! I was mad enough to do 'most anything to him, but—"

Adams pounded the top of his desk. "You'll get your chance to talk later, young man. Sit down."

Ed Mabry was called. His testimony substantiated that of the first witness. Other witnesses told of the fight in the Long Branch, started by Shand; some of them had heard him say to Culley then, "I ought to kill you!" and so testified.

Then Jerry Shand took the chair. Adams looked at him sternly. "You've heard the testimony that you threatened to kill the victim. A barful of people saw you pick a fight with him. What you got to say?"

"I don't deny any of that," Shand said tensely, "except that when I said it, I said it in anger and I didn't actually intend to kill him. I shot him, all right, but I shot him in self-defense. He pulled a gun on me."

"Marshal Matt Dillon ain't here right now," Adams said, "but he's told me no gun was found—I mean no gun that Culley had, or is claimed to have had. That's that. The next point is—why would Andy Culley want to shoot you?"

"He wanted to shut me up. He didn't want me telling how he'd been a bushwhacker with Quantrill. You saw the tattoo on his arm!"

"Tattoo don't make a man a bushwhacker," snapped Adams.

"This one does!" Shand retorted. "I saw it on his arm, when they came for my father and mother. That was in Lawrence. That's why I'm sure. They—killed both of them . . . and then they went across the street to where my girl

lived, and they took her away. I never saw her again . . ."
His voice trailed off, his face hard.

There was a commotion at the front door. Heads turned; Adams bent a fierce gaze at the two people there. Jerry Shand stared.

Belle Archer was a step in front of Matt Dillon. The marshal's right hand cupped her elbow. Belle wore a pretty, bright-colored gown, but her face was drawn and miserable.

Jerry Shand stood up, his mouth slightly open, his eyes wide. Belle Archer took a halting step forward.

"Hello—Jerry," she said huskily.

"Lord!" Jerry Shand breathed. Then: "Ellie . . . ?"

"Belle Archer, now . . ." She paused, fumbled for words. "Matt says either I—talk, or they take you away. If it wasn't for that, I wouldn't do this to you, Jerry. You've had it bad enough already. I—didn't want you to see me now . . . see what happened to Ellie Clark after that day in Lawrence."

"Just a minute, now!" Doc Adams interjected. "What's this all about, Matt?"

"I believe Miss Archer's got some testimony to give, Doc. What she has to say ought to be controlling in this case."

"All right, then!" Adams said with asperity. "Put her on the stand—no need to make a show out of these proceedings!"

Shand was excused from the stand and Belle was sworn in. Adams asked a couple of preliminary questions and then told her to go ahead with any pertinent information.

"I can tell you all about last night, Doc," she said simply. Her eyes swung to Jerry Shand, who was watching her unblinkingly, his face masking whatever emotion he was feeling. "I left the Long Branch early last night—left because I saw Jerry coming in. I didn't want him to see me. I went home—to my room, I mean. And I saw everything that happened from my window—between Jerry and Andy Culley. I saw Andy pull a gun out of his pocket and point it at Jerry. Then Jerry drew his gun and fired—but he *had* to do it, Doc, or he would've been killed!"

She stopped. Doc Adams took his eyes from her and looked at the accused man. Jerry Shand's eyes were brimming with tears.

"What Jerry told Matt was true, Doc," she ended. "I saw it all . . . And I saw that fool Busby kid pick up Andy's gun and run away with it." Amid silence, she left the witness chair. Gently, Matt took her arm and led her to the door.

Marshal Matt Dillon stood in front of his office, patting the neck of Jerry Shand's saddled horse. Jerry toed the stirrup and swung aboard. He looked down at the lawman.

"I—I don't know how I . . ." he began.

"It's over and done with," Matt said quietly. "Forget it now."

"Yeah," Jerry said.

"Better get going, Jerry," Matt said gravely.

"I wish I could see Ellie first . . ."

"It's like I said before—she refuses to see you, Jerry."

"I don't figure why Ellie—it don't seem right she won't!"

"Listen. She said to tell you Ellie's gone . . ."

"Gone?" Jerry stared at him.

"Yes, gone. She means she isn't Ellie Clark any more—at least, the Ellie Clark you knew. Remember, she's been through a lot, Jerry—maybe more than you have, even. It's a rough life she leads—but she likes it, now. She couldn't share a different kind of one with you. She might pretend, but she couldn't fool you long, and she's smart enough to know it. And big enough to want to spare you.

"It's true, kid. Ellie's gone. There's only Belle Archer." Matt looked up at Jerry Shand for a long moment. Then he lifted a hand.

"So long, Jerry."

Jerry Shand raised his own hand and let it drop. "So long, Marshal." His voice was almost inaudible. He reined his horse around and touched spurs.

ROAD RANCH

Matt Dillon and his deputy, Chester Proudfoot, were pleasantly engaged in digesting their supper. Sprawled on tilted-back chairs in front of the marshal's office, they saw a man hurrying toward them in the dusk. They sat erect.

"Ain't that the stage driver?" Chester said.

"It's Jim Buck, all right," Matt affirmed. "Howdy, Jim," he greeted as the man came near.

"Howdy, Marshal . . . Chester." He seemed excited.

"Trouble, Jim?" Matt asked.

"Worser'n trouble, Marshal—got held up, one passenger shot down in cold blood—as mean a thing's I ever did see."

"Where did it happen?"

"Other side of Wagon Bed Springs—between there and Daggett's."

"Daggett's . . . ?" Matt couldn't place the name.

"Jesse Daggett—he runs the stage station out near the Coloradder line. Don't trust that man, I don't."

"What do you mean, Jim?"

"I suspicion he's in on this—Jesse Daggett, I mean. He knew I was carryin' a little gold. We lay over there, ye know; and whilst we was doin' so I seen Daggett talkin' private to a gent who'd just rode in, a hard-lookin' cuss."

"Then what, Jim?"

"Feller rode off, left afore we did. Looks to me like he changed his hoss and outfit somewheres near by and waited for us."

"You mean the man who held you up was riding a different horse and wearing different clothes, but you think it was the same man you saw talking to Daggett earlier?"

"That's just what I mean! He was all alone. Had his face covered with a mask. Never said a word. Took the box, robbed the passengers. Then he mounted up, ready to ride off, but before he did he shot one of the passengers—Ryerson, that drummer from St. Louis—right in the head!"

Matt looked at the shaken driver. "Ryerson had made no move—wasn't going for a hide-out gun or anything?"

"No sir, by Godfreys! Now why'd a man do a thing like

25

that, Marshal? It don't make sense; didn't say a word, didn't cuss him or nothin', like he might've had somethin' agin the man. Just shot him down like a dog."

"He just likes to kill, maybe—one of that breed. I'll ride back to Daggett's with you tomorrow, Jim. Talk to him."

"Didn't have nobody ridin' gun," Jim Buck said regretfully. "Figgered it'd give it away I was carryin' gold if I did . . ."

"Don't let it weigh on your mind, Jim," Matt said. "See you in the morning."

The next day Matt and Chester rode Jim Buck's stage on the return trip to Daggett's station. It was a full day's trip, with a stop at Wagon Bed Springs, and Matt, who had ridden topside with Jim Buck all the way, was glad to see Daggett's. It was a typical road-ranch stage stop with a big dining room and a row of cubicles for travelers.

Matt got his first chance to talk to Daggett in the yard after supper had been eaten. Jesse Daggett was a tall, angular man with a gaunt, lined face. He seemed quiet and contained but Matt thought he sensed an inner tension in him.

"Cold weather'll be coming soon," he said, making talk. "Have to lay in some more whisky."

Matt asked him how long he had been running the station.

"Three years, come spring. Put it up myself," he said, with a touch of pride. "Pawnees've made a couple tries to burn her down, but I'm still here."

"And you're planning on staying here, aren't you, Daggett?"

"A man's plans are his own, Marshal," Daggett responded with some asperity.

So the man was touchy, Matt thought. He'd have to handle him carefully if he was going to get anywhere.

"No offense," he said quietly. Daggett looked mollified, and he added, "Think I'd like it here myself—no neighbors to bother you but lots of company passing through."

"Company." Daggett sniffed, as though he didn't exactly savor the thought.

"All kinds of people on the road," Matt offered. Then, tentatively: "Some good and some bad."

"True," the station keeper said, glancing quickly at Matt.

"That fellow who held up Jim Buck and shot the passenger . . ."

Daggett said quietly, "One of the bad ones, all right—killin' in cold blood that way."

"You don't figure it could have been a mistake, Daggett? That his gun might have gone off accidentally?"

"Sure," Daggett said sardonically; "anything's possible."

"I take it from your tone of voice that you don't think it did," Matt said politely.

"What I think about it ain't likely to bring back the dead," Daggett said sourly.

"No, it won't," Matt said. He laid a direct gaze on the man. "But it might keep other people from dying."

The man said nothing while he pulled out a pipe and stuffed it full of rough-cut. "Figgered that's what you come down for, Marshal—lookin' for that fellow." He struck a match and held it over the pipe bowl.

"No secret about that," Matt told him.

He finished lighting, tossed the match away, took a couple of long puffs. "All right, Marshal. You're welcome to stay as long as you like."

"It could take quite a while."

"What you're paid for," Daggett admitted.

Matt decided the man was settling into a calmer mood. He said, "Buck thinks maybe it was the man he saw talking to you here that day."

Daggett thought a minute. "Nat Pilcher, that was." He took a breath and added slowly, "Marshal, I don't care what Jim Buck thinks."

Matt probed the statement for meaning but its implication eluded him. He'd have to try another tack.

"It hurts the stage company's business when passengers get shot," he said. "If any more get shot near here, it will hurt yours."

"It will for a fact, Marshal."

Matt felt that he was getting somewhere. "Stage holdups happen, everybody expects it. The stage company discounts it; the law handles them on a matter-of-course enforcement basis. But shooting someone down for no reason . . . you figure this man's a born killer?"

"I ain't saying it was Pilcher, Marshal. But whoever it was, he could've had a lot of reasons, maybe."

Matt said, "Sure," and waited expectantly. The station keeper seemed to be opening up.

"Men are all different," Daggett went on. "They got different reasons for doin' what they do, for livin' the way they live. I reckon it's what happened to 'em in the past that makes it so."

Matt rolled a cigarette. "Yeah. That's why I'm a lawman. Why you run a stage station. Why this man—whoever it was—holds up a stage . . . and kills in cold blood."

Daggett said nothing while Matt lit up and drew in the smoke. The silence ran on long enough for him to finish half his cigarette. Finally the other seemed to come to a decision. He straightened and knocked the dottle from his pipe.

"Marshal, I've got just one thing to tell you. It's this: I believe in letting every man kill his own snakes."

Matt snubbed out his cigarette. "I take it you mean that this killing is mine to solve without your help, is that it?"

"That's the size of it, Marshal. I won't interfere with you—but I won't help you."

"Well, Daggett, I think that you know something you could tell me if you would. I don't have to tell you this is serious business—an innocent man has been killed. It's my job to apprehend the killer. It's every good citizen's job to help me as much as he can. In the circumstances, your philosophy doesn't impress me much, mister."

"It's got to be that way," was the stubborn response. "Let dog eat dog, I say."

"All right, Daggett," Matt said calmly. "I hope you're not going to regret this . . ."

"I've had a lot of regrets in my life, Marshal. One more ain't going to break me."

In spite of the disappointing interview with Jesse Daggett, Matt shied away from sharing Jim Buck's continued suspicion of the man. Buck was sure that he was partners with the road agent. The station keeper's refusal to confirm or deny the charge that Pilcher was the holdup-killer puzzled Matt. It could be that he simply didn't know . . . but if that was the case why didn't the man come right out and say so? But if he did know, and was Pilcher's accomplice, why had he admitted knowing the man at all? Somehow, Daggett didn't seem to fit the role of criminal. Matt knew that mere appearances could not be trusted in his business, but he was relying on a deep intuitive sense that had in the past rarely betrayed him.

But right now the only lead he had to work on was Jim

Buck's suspicion of Daggett. If it was well founded, Pilcher ought to be hanging around in the vicinity and might show up again at the station. He had Chester keep vigil there while he borrowed a horse from Daggett and covered the region around in a saddleback search. By the afternoon of the second day he had given up the effort to spot Pilcher's supposed hide-out nearby. He and Chester were listlessly playing two-handed stud in the station when, toward dusk, Jim Buck's stage pulled in from the west. His passengers headed for their rooms to clean up. Buck came in while Daggett was still in the yard, seeing that his halfbreed hostler got the horses taken care of. The driver came over to Matt and Chester.

"Howdy, boys. Wish I had an easy job like yours."

"Howdy, Jim," Matt responded with a smile.

"What you mean, easy?" Chester demanded. "Don't you be fooled because we sit around like this. We do a lot of thinkin', an' that makes up for it."

"You do, eh?" Buck snorted. "Well, ye done any 'bout locatin' old man Daggett's sidekick?"

"You mean Nat Pilcher, I guess," Matt said. "I'm not sure we want to find him, Jim—he could've been just a cowboy riding through."

"Yeah," Buck said and spat at a cuspidor. "Anyways, I got no gold this trip, so I ain't got anythin' to worry about."

"That's good, Jim." Matt turned his head at the sound of a horse approaching. The clop of hoofs slowed and stopped. "Pilgrim for supper, sounds like."

"Man's gotta be danged hungry to ride in here to eat," Buck said. "Daggett's food's mighty shy on quality." He started for the rear. "Got to check on that hostler. Don't trust him—ner Daggett neither."

"Hard work, drivin' stage," Chester said to Matt after Buck had disappeared. "Wouldn't want to do that for a livin'."

The front door opened and a dust-covered man entered. He was of middle height and stocky build. Cold blue eyes crowded a too-big nose. A week-old stubble covered his jaw. He stood there indolently, regarding the pair at the table, and an unpleasant grin cracked his face.

"Heard they was a marshal here," he grunted.

"That's me," Matt said, "Matt Dillon, out of Dodge City. What can I do for you?"

The grin stayed there. "You can't do nothin' for me, Marshal. I just wanted to see what a marshal looks like—a live one, I mean."

Matt stood up. He was watching the newcomer, but he was aware that Chester had pushed back from the table enough so that his right arm was free. Chester was a little dumb in some ways but he was a good gun. Matt was confidently aware of what he himself could do. There was probably no real cause for concern here anyway. The man might be a fool but more likely he was just a big-mouth.

"You see me," Matt said. "Satisfied?"

"Sure," he said; "sure, I'm satisfied."

"Then get out of here," Matt said.

The grin was wiped off. "Now you sound touchy," he said complainingly. "You sound real touchy, Marshal. I ain't tryin' to start no trouble. I just come in here to say howdy, friendly-like."

Scorn shone for a moment in the marshal's eyes. "What's your go-by, mister?"

"Name's Pilcher," came the answer. "Nat Pilcher."

Matt flicked a glance at Chester. The deputy pushed back farther from the table. "I've heard about you," Matt said.

"Sure," Pilcher said. "Jesse Daggett's an old friend of mine."

"Where've you been hanging your hat, Pilcher? Got a job around here?"

"I'm ridin' the grub line right now, Marshal. Know anybody 'round here that needs a good hand?"

Matt pretended to consider this. "Do you do anything besides ride, Pilcher?" he asked.

Pilcher's grin came back. "Now it's funny you ask that."

"Tell me why," Matt said.

"You bein' a lawman, I mean . . . you ever heard o' Charlie Haw, over in New Mex'?"

Matt looked at him. "I've heard of Charlie, yes."

"Well, old Charlie got hisself shot recent. They're sayin' Clay Allison shot him." The grin widened. "I know for a fact, though, it wasn't Clay . . ." He stepped back, felt behind him for the latch, and swung the door open. "See you later, Marshal—if you're gonna hang around." He went out.

Chester looked at Matt. "Doggone," he said, "what'd the poison pup mean by all that?"

"He means that he isn't afraid of me, Chester," Matt

said. "And he also means that if I had any sense I'd be afraid of him."

Chester chuckled. "You got any sense, Mr. Dillon?"

"Sense enough to be wary of a mad dog, Chester. And I'm just as happy that my back wasn't turned when he came in."

"I wouldn't let him shoot you in the back, Mr. Dillon!"

"Thank you, Chester," Matt said.

Despite Nat Pilcher's farewell comment, Matt and Chester saw no more of the man that night. The next morning early Jim Buck loaded his passengers back on the stage for Dodge, and climbed to the driver's seat and popped his long whip over the lead team's heads. The coach rolled away. Matt stood in the yard with Jesse Daggett and watched the moving cloud of dust.

"Well, he'll make Dodge tonight," Daggett remarked, "and be back here tomorrow night."

"Yeah," Matt said; "if he don't get shot up."

"No reason he should," Daggett responded. "No gold in the express box this trip."

Matt glanced at him. "Met your friend Pilcher last night."

"Funny thing," the station keeper said. "He come in near supper time and I figgered he wanted a meal but he rode off again without eatin'."

"Looks like he came in just to tell me what a hard case he is," Matt offered. "Sort of a warning."

"I notice you're still here," Daggett said drily.

"I don't scare quite that easy."

"You're all right, Marshal"—he said it grudgingly—"but you ought to go back to Dodge."

"Why should I, Daggett?"

"Things'll work out here," he said doggedly; "without you, I mean."

"Go ahead, man—say what's on your mind!"

The answer came in a growl. "Nope, that's all; there's nothin' more to say."

"Listen, Daggett. I'm not meddling in your affairs. There's been a holdup. And a murder."

"You accusin' me, Dillon?"

"No, I'm not. I've got no evidence for doing that. And frankly I don't even share Jim Buck's suspicions about you; I believe you're an honest man."

Daggett's strained expression relaxed. "Thanks, Marshal—thanks for that."

"All right," Matt said. "But I still don't propose to go back to Dodge till I've got the guilty man. It might be Nat Pilcher—and I think it will be. If you could help me prove it is him, and you don't . . . well, I hope your reasons are mighty good ones, Daggett."

"I've said it before," Daggett responded in a low voice; "every man's got his reasons for what he does."

"I won't press it any more, Daggett." Matt looked around the yard. "You ought to plant some trees here. Improve the place."

"Not enough water," Daggett said shortly.

"Dig for it." Matt told him. "It looks barren and cheerless here. A few trees would smarten it up."

"It doesn't bother me. Passengers don't mind it—except a woman going through once in a while . . ."

"Speaking of women, were you ever married, Daggett?"

"I come close once. That was back in New Mexico . . . a long time ago. A fine woman, Dillon, but I—lost her. I been lonely ever since."

Matt was touched by the sadness in the man's voice. "I'm sorry."

"Funny how a man goes on livin'—when it don't seem there's anything left to him to live for . . . Come on in, I'll get you some breakfast."

Chester was restive the next day so Matt sent him out to scout around the country while the marshal himself stayed at the station. "I don't reckon there's much chance you'll stumble onto anything," he told the deputy, "but if there's anybody besides Pilcher hanging around the Trail between here and Wagon Bed I want to know it." Matt spent the day in the company of Daggett, who proved amiably willing to discuss such topics as the buffalo slaughter and how to outsmart the Indians but took refuge in generalities every time Matt tried to bring the subject around to stage holdups.

Chester rode back in to the station, tired and dusty, well before sunset. One look at his face told Matt his deputy had drawn a zero. Chester went to wash up and take a nap. Daggett, who was currently without kitchen help, started to make preparations for supper, and Matt settled down to await the stage's arrival.

Chester showed up, rubbing his eyes, just as Matt heard the wheel-rumble and hoof-pound from the east. They went out front together. The 'breed hostler, showing up from the corral as the big vehicle pulled to a halt, grabbed the off leader's bridle. Matt saw that something was wrong and legged it the last few yards to the stage as Jim Buck slid awkwardly down from the seat.

"More trouble, Jim?" he asked.

The driver glared at him from reddened eyes, swaying on his feet as he stood there. His left shoulder showed blood-stain.

"He done it agin, Marshal! And cripes, if you don't take out after him now *I'm* goin' to! Just you look in the coach!"

"In a minute . . . you hit bad, Jim?"

"Naw, just a nick. Knocked me plumb off the box, though. I wasn't goin' to stop—but that stopped me. The hosses would've bolted, but I managed to hold onto the ribbons. . . . Now look into that coach, I say!"

Matt did as he was told. He stared at the crumpled body for a long moment; then he touched the cooling, lifeless wrist. He swung back and looked at Jim Buck. The driver glared back at him.

"A woman, Jim . . ."

"You saw her, Marshal . . . *he* killed her! That's all he done, after the stage stopped. Rode up, with me there on the ground, hangin' onto them ribbons an' yellin' at the hosses, and put a bullet in her and rode off . . ."

Chester peered into the coach. He turned away quickly, face white and lips clamped, to stare at Matt.

"Where's the rest of your passengers, Jim?" Matt asked.

"Wa'n't none—she was the lone one this trip. Look at her, Marshal!"

"Do you think it was Pilcher, Jim?"

"I know it was the same one as the other day—and who else could it 'a' been but Pilcher? The lowdown, murderin' skunk!" He raised his voice: "Where's Daggett? *Hey, Daggett!*"

Slow footsteps approached, and Matt knew without looking that Daggett had emerged from the station.

"Ask Jesse Daggett who it was," Buck said bitterly to Matt. Then to the station keeper: "Take a look inside the coach, damn you—a good look . . ."

When Daggett turned back to them, having taken his look his face was haggard and brittle.

"What d'you think of that, Daggett—murderin' a woman?" Jim Buck challenged.

Daggett looked like a man dazed and unhearing. Without a word, he headed for the station, walking slowly, his shoulders slumped.

"Look at him," Jim Buck said scathingly. "Look at the durn buzzard . . . ever see a guiltier-lookin' man in yore life?"

"Jim, you're wrong," Matt said. "It can't be . . ."

"He didn't do it, I know that!" Jim Buck snapped. "But he's in on it . . . somehow."

"Chester," Matt said, "help me carry the body inside. Then we'll see what we can do about that shoulder of yours, Jim."

He and the deputy toted the woman into the stage station. Then Matt dressed and bandaged Jim Buck's shoulder. The wound was not a bad one but Matt, fearing a possible infection, did it with care and it took time. Chester helped him, Daggett having disappeared. Matt wondered where he had gone but assumed he was helping the hostler care for the team.

Then they had to see about the woman. Jim Buck wasn't sure who she was. She hadn't started from Dodge, he said; she was a through passenger from Kansas City, bound for Santa Fe. It was possible that she was going out there to meet a prospective husband but from her appearance Matt judged it was more likely that she was a honkytonk girl heading for a new job. They could find out the details later. The weather was warm and they couldn't take chances; he and Chester dug a shallow grave and buried her under a rude cross.

By that time it was nearing dark. Daggett still had not shown up. Matt questioned the hostler, who said that his employer had saddled a horse and ridden away while they were taking care of Jim Buck. Matt, hurrying back inside, ascertained that the station keeper had taken his gun. He broke the news to Chester.

"We'll have to hit saddle and try to pick up his tracks before it's full dark."

"You figger he's gone to find Pilcher?" the deputy asked.

"That's what I think, Chester."

He questioned the hostler further while the horses were being made ready. The man had not bothered to notice which way Daggett had lined out. However, Chester spotted fresh hoofprints within a few minutes. They followed them long enough for Matt to determine that the station keeper was making a beeline for a low mesa to the northwest. He and Chester headed that way as the darkness deepened around them.

"I circled that mesa the other day," Matt remarked, "but I didn't see any hoof sign around there."

"I wasn't far away from it myself, today," Chester admitted. "I didn't spot nothing either, but the ground's mighty hard over there and I didn't do no close lookin'."

"Could be we haven't been very smart, Chester—it's the one high spot around here where he could watch the trail and keep tabs on our movements too."

"How long a start you think Daggett had on us?"

"Long enough," Matt said sourly. "More than an hour—hour and a half, anyway."

Talk languished. They kept their ponies at a trot. Time and distance passed while Matt worried. He recalled Daggett's declaration that a man should kill his own snakes. He judged it probable that the station keeper, who somehow felt forced to tolerate other crimes, had been incensed by the wanton killing of the woman. If he was now going out after Pilcher on his own, he was courting danger, Matt thought, as he was unable to consider Daggett as being handy with a gun.

They finally got close enough to the mesa to discern it looming above them. They stopped the horses long enough to check their guns, then proceeded slowly.

They found Daggett twenty minutes later, in a narrow *rincon* that fissured the west side of the mesa, its entrance concealed by brush. They were guided to it by intermittent moaning and by the lingering glow of what had been Nat Pilcher's cookfire. Daggett was lying fifteen feet away from it, in a slowly widening pool of his life blood. They found the station keeper's horse stamping nervously some yards away. There was no sign of Pilcher, though, or of his horse.

After a quick examination of the man, Matt tried to make him comfortable for his final minutes. It was all he could do. Daggett was mortally hurt. His low moaning stopped, and he seemed to become aware of their presence.

"Marshal—?" he said in a husky whisper. At Matt's murmured assent, he said, "You followed me . . . ?"

"Where's Pilcher?" Matt asked. "What happened?"

"I could have killed him," Daggett said. "I had my gun on him before he heard me—but I couldn't shoot him in the back, low as he was . . ."

"You let him draw on you, man?" Matt asked fiercely.

"Let him see me," Daggett admitted. "Knew—he was a fast gun, but I let him—see me before I pulled trigger. I was a fool . . . got off one shot before he could—but I hurried it . . . missed . . . he didn't . . . no luck left at all . . ." His voice trailed off.

"Any idea where he went?"

"Said he was going back to station . . . get you . . ."

"I'd have come with you, Daggett."

"Not your business, Marshal . . . this between him and me . . . you know?"

"Tell me, Daggett."

"Back in New Mexico, it started," Daggett said, and groaned. Matt waited. The man went on, in a whisper punctuated by gasps. "Three, four years . . . ago. I shot and killed a man . . . it was self-defense, him or me, but I couldn't prove that. He was . . . pal of Pilcher's, and Pilcher swore he'd gun me down. I heard, and pulled stakes . . . I wasn't no gunman, didn't want trouble . . ."

He groaned. Matt and Chester waited. "He found me . . . last week. I thought he'd kill me. But he'd cooled off. Just threatened to expose me. I'm still under indictment . . . back in New Mexico. He's been holdin' up stages for years, makes his livin' doing that . . . But he's kill-crazy too; that man a few days back I could stand for—but not a woman, Marshal . . . the woman I lost was killed by a drunken fool shootin' wild on the street. I saw red then . . ."

"I could have stopped this if you'd told me sooner, Daggett," Matt said.

"I was . . . afraid. And every man . . . kill own snakes . . . but you can have him now . . . I ain't going to . . ."

"I'm going after him." Matt stood up. "I'm sorry, Daggett. Chester can stay here with you."

"Both of you . . . go," he said weakly. "I ain't afraid . . . die alone."

"So long, Daggett," Matt said.

"Good-by, Marshal . . ."

Matt led Chester a few steps away. "Stay here with him.
Do what you can for him. It won't be much."

"Okay," Chester said. "The poor feller."

"I'll send that hostler out to help you bring him in later,"
Matt said, and mounted. "Better hobble that horse of his so
it don't stray. You'll need it." He swung his own animal's
head. "So long, Chester."

"So long, Marshal," Chester said. "You watch it, now."

There was a light in the main room of the stage station but
Matt could hear no sound, discern no movement in or around
the place. Fifty yards out he left saddle and approached on
foot, slowly. He reached a spot from where he could look
into the lighted window. He could see no one. He circled
the main building. When he was a few yards from the small
barn a low whistle halted him. He keened the darkness,
waiting. The whistle came again.

"Jim . . . ?" he said in a low voice.

Jim Buck came out of the barn. "Over here, Matt."

Matt went to his side. "Pilcher here somewhere?"

"In the station."

"I couldn't spot him," Matt said.

"Back in the kitchen, lookin' fer Daggett's whisky. You
find Daggett?"

"Yes—with Pilcher's bullet in him. He's dying, may be
dead by now. Chester stayed with him. What happened
here?"

"Pilcher sneaked up, got the drop on me. Took my gun,
told me to stay put inside but I skinned out when he went
prowlin' fer whisky."

"Where's the 'breed?"

"Dunno. Thought he'd be out here but I couldn't find him.
Skeered off, I reckon. What you aim to do, Matt?"

"Go in and arrest Pilcher for murder," Matt Dillon said,
and started for the main building.

He peered into the lighted window again, closer to it this
time. As he did so the door to the kitchen swung open. Pilcher
strode into the room, a jug in one hand and a satisfied look
on his face. He looked around the room and saw that Jim
Buck had gone. He dropped the jug with a curse, eased the
gun in his holster, and headed for the front door.

Matt, catfooting swiftly, was ten feet away from the door
when it swung open. Light spilled out, but Matt was safely

to one side of it. Pilcher hung back, refusing to show himself in the illuminated doorway. He was a killer but he knew the uses of caution.

"Hey, driver!" he called. "Show yourself!"

Matt gestured to Jim Buck, behind him. "Out here I'm safe," Jim called back. "I aim to stay here."

"Come on back in here!" Pilcher ordered. "Heck, I won't hurt you; I just want to keep an eye on you."

"You want me in there, you better come get me!" Jim Buck said.

Pilcher was silent for a moment. Matt could picture his face as he examined this problem, pale eyes narrowed.

"You see any sign of that lawman or his pet rabbit?" Pilcher asked guilelessly.

"If I had I'd be gittin' ready to dance on yore grave," Jim Buck said. "No such luck . . ."

Matt heard Pilcher give a little chuckle. "Well, c'mon back in," he wheedled. "I found us a jug."

Jim Buck hesitated, until Matt nodded his head vigorously. "Wal, all right," the driver said; "I could use a snort."

Slowly he walked around the marshal, toward the door. When he was two steps from it, the killer appeared in the opening. His gun was in his hand. Jim Buck paused. Pilcher, seeing that the driver's unbandaged arm was carrying no weapon possibly picked up in the barn, let the muzzle of his own gun sag. He moved his head in a curt signal for Buck to enter as he stood aside. Buck entered the building.

"Lead me to that jug!" he said hoarsely. The strain was beginning to tell on him, Matt realized.

"Dang it, I ought to lay your scalp open!" Pilcher complained, but to Matt's relief he let his gun drop back into its holster.

Matt eased out his own Colt's and took a step forward.

Pilcher, reaching for the latch to swing the door closed, caught Matt's movement. He straightened, reached for his gun again.

"Hold it!" Matt said.

Pilcher froze. He peered at the figure before the door, still partly in the dark. Matt took another step and stood full in the beam of light. He let Pilcher get a good look at the gun he was holding. The muzzle was pointed at the killer's middle.

Pilcher's voice was steady. "Been out ridin', Marshal?"

"Yes, I have," Matt said. "So have you."

"Man like me rides a lot, Marshal."

"This time you should have kept riding," Matt told him.

"Well, now, Marshal, I wanted to see you agin before I left," Pilcher said.

There was no change in the man's voice. Matt Dillon felt an instant's small wonder at his aplomb, then lost it: he'd seen a dozen like this man, callous killers who knew no fear or, if they did, had schooled themselves well in hiding it.

"Daggett told me that," he said.

"Yeah?" Pilcher grated. "Did the skunk tell you I was goin' to shoot you, too?"

"Jesse Daggett was a good man, Pilcher," Matt said.

"He was a murderin' sidewinder!" Pilcher's voice rose. "He killed the best friend I ever had!"

Matt saw that Pilcher was working himself up to the point where he might make a desperate try for his gun. "That's enough palaver," he told the man quietly. "I'm arresting you for murder, Pilcher."

"The devil," Pilcher said. "Ain't you going to give me a fightin' chance, now?"

"I'm not paid to engage in duels. I'm paid to enforce the law," Matt said. "I've got the drop on you, so just unbuckle that gunbelt and let it fall. You can take your chances in court."

"I figger my chances are better right here, Dillon." His right arm tensed. "You ain't shootin' no settin' duck!"

Matt felt sweat break out on his brow. "Don't make a fool play!" he warned.

Pilcher's hand flashed to his gun and up. He was fast, terribly fast, but Matt's bullet hit him before he pulled trigger. He kept his feet long enough to get off one wide shot. Matt fired again. Pilcher sagged against the doorframe and slid to the floor.

Matt holstered his gun. He was trembling. Nat Pilcher had been a rotten specimen of manhood but still he had been a human being, presumably with some spark of decency hidden deep within him. Now no one would ever find it. . . .

Jim Buck stepped across the dead man and saw that Matt was unharmed. "Gosh," he said, "I never thought he'd try it."

"It was a fool play," Matt Dillon said.

GRASS

Matt Dillon was thinking that Harry Pope was a long way from home, and not only in a geographical sense. Other men, a good many of them, had come from the East to Kansas and demonstrated their fitness to survive in a new, hard environment. A few of them even flourished and prospered in it. But not Harry Pope. The man just didn't fit in, out here on the prairie.

Sitting in his chair, Matt studied the man as he stood at the bar, shifting his weight nervously from foot to foot as he sipped at his beer. Pope was a short man, slim to the point of frailness. Matt judged he'd be better off clerking behind a counter in some department store back in Boston, which was where Chester said the young man had come from.

"Yeah," the marshal said quietly, "he's come a long, long way from home. Can't figure what prodded him to come out here."

"Well," Chester offered, "his wife died and he couldn't stand it there any more, couldn't forget her. So out West he come. Been here about four months, built himself a soddy a few miles out. He's planted some corn, and he's tryin' to raise pigs!" Chester sounded slightly scandalized.

"Not much of a corn country," Matt said. "Still, Pete Kitchen raised garden truck and pigs in Arizona."

"Pope's got a little water there. A real farmer could make out, I suppose, but he don't know any more about farmin' than I do—prob'ly not as much. Besides," Chester said, "he's scared to death."

"He tell you that, Chester?"

"Yeah, a couple times. I wish you'd talk to him; maybe you could get him straightened out."

The deputy was plainly worried about this pilgrim from Boston. Matt realized that Chester wasn't going to be satisfied until Matt talked to the fellow. Still, he wasn't anxious to do so.

"I doubt if anybody could do that," he said. "From what you've told me, his trouble's all in his head."

40

Chester chose to interpret that as consent. He raised his voice: "Pope . . . hey, Mr. Pope!" He lifted his hand as Harry Pope looked back toward them. "Over here . . ."

Pope walked slowly to their table. "Hello, Chester," he said in a low, not unpleasant voice.

"This here's Marshal Dillon," Chester said. "Harry Pope."

"Howdy, Pope. Sit down." Matt nodded at an empty chair.

"Glad to meet you, Marshal." Harry Pope perched himself on the chair's edge.

"Chester tells me something's got you worried, Pope. What seems to be the trouble?"

"It's those Indians coming around the place at night, Marshal. Yelling and whooping to wake the dead."

Matt stared at the man. He wasn't trying to hurraw Matt; his face was pale and he was in dead earnest.

"How often do they do this?" he asked carefully. "Every night?"

"Oh, no. Once a week or so."

"Sure they're Indians making the racket? Couldn't be coyotes?"

"Good heavens, I know what coyotes sound like, Marshal, even if I am a tenderfoot! It's human voices I hear."

"Well, what are the voices saying?"

"Nothing I can understand, you know—just insane screeching and yodeling. I don't see why the Army can't send some soldiers out and drive them off. If they catch me outside the house just once, I'll be done for."

"Pope, I don't think you've been hearing Indians. If it was Indians, you'd have been done for by now. But they just don't operate that way, whooping and yelling outside your door, warning you not to come out. You've heard a lot of stories that have alarmed you, and your imagination has done the rest." Matt smiled at him reassuringly.

"Oh no, it's Indians all right—and *I've heard them!*"

Matt felt mildly exasperated with the greenhorn. "Well, why don't you shoot 'em?" he asked indulgently.

Pope's voice was small. "I—don't have a gun, Marshal."

"Know how to handle one?" Matt barked.

"Yes, I do," the greenhorn averred. "I did quite a lot of shooting back East. But I didn't bring a gun with me when I came out here, and I've hesitated to get one—afraid it would make things worse."

"Anyone needs a gun around here," Matt told him. "Get one. Then if they come around again, use it."

"But if I shot one of them, wouldn't that get the whole tribe on my neck?"

"Oh I don't think so, Pope. I wouldn't worry any about that if I was you."

"All right then, I'll do it. I'll get a gun today and take it home with me. It's been nice talking to you, Marshal; good day, and thanks. Good day, Chester."

"So long, Pope." Matt watched the little man go out, his thin shoulders straightened in an attempt to show that he was no longer a man afraid. The marshal glanced at Chester, winked, and shook his head.

Four days later, seated behind his desk, Matt Dillon was staring incredulously at Ned Honeyman, whose ranch, a few miles out of Dodge City, bordered on Harry Pope's homestead claim.

"What d'you mean: Pope is a killer?" he demanded.

"I mean he shot and killed Joe Carter last night!" Honeyman said loudly. "Carter's worked for me for years, one of the best men I ever had! No more, though—that danged homesteader saw to that!"

"How'd it happen, Ned? Was there a fight?"

"Fight my eye! Pope shot Joe in cold blood—near that tumbledown soddy of his. Never give Joe a chance! I crave to see him hang!"

"You see it happen, Ned?"

"Not me, but Earl Brant was there, he seen it. Brought Joe back to the ranch. Earl works for me too, you know."

"I know," Matt said. "What did Brant have to say about it?"

"Why, just that they was ridin' by the stinkin' sodbuster's hut and he bust out and shot Joe and killed him!"

"Ned," Matt said slowly, thinking of the talk he'd had with Harry Pope at Chester's instigation, "this whole thing could have been a sorry mistake."

"Mistake!" Ire pinked Honeyman's cheeks, popped his eyes. "Durn it, you going out there to arrest that feller or not?"

"I'll ride out there in the morning, Ned," Matt told him calmly. "Harry Pope isn't likely to run away."

His confidence was rewarded the next day. He and Chester

saw signs of someone's presence as they approached Pope's homestead although they did not spot the Easterner immediately. It didn't look like much of a place, the sodhouse small and rickety-looking, the lines of fence ill-made and awkward-looking. Matt reminded himself the man was a rank tenderfoot, completely unprepared for this kind of venture.

"There he is," Chester said as they rode closer in; "over by the pigpen."

They reined over to the crude enclosure. Matt's horse fidgeted at the unfamiliar smell of the porkers. He stepped the horse around so as to get upwind. Pope turned to face them and Matt gave him a howdy.

"Good morning, Marshal . . . Chester," he said. He looked more composed than when Matt had seen him last. "Well, they came back again—night before last."

"Who do you mean, Pope?"

"Those Indians I told you about. But I'd got that gun you told me to get, and I used it. Scared 'em off, I guess. For good, I hope."

"How many—uh—Indians were there, d'you know?" Matt asked.

"Two, I guess—that's all I saw, anyway."

"And you used your gun on 'em, eh? Hit one of 'em?"

"That I don't know. I certainly tried, but it was too dark to see if I scored a hit or not."

Matt dismounted and Chester followed suit. "Tell me all about it, Pope," Matt invited him.

"All right, but first won't you come in and have some coffee?" Matt said they would, and Chester tended to the horses while the others got settled inside the little soddy.

"It began like the other times," Pope said while Matt sipped coffee and watched the Easterner. "Yelling and whooping outside, they were. I put out my lamp and got my gun. Then I opened the door a crack and yelled at *them*. They screeched back and fired a couple of shots at the house. The bullets went high but they thudded into the wall. They didn't hit anywhere near the door so I opened it wider and I heard a horse off over to the west, and I saw something moving dimly. I let loose two shots and then another began shooting from somewhere else so I ducked back inside. I waited but they didn't do anything more—didn't even yell again. They seem to have gone away right afterward. I don't believe they were very wild Indians."

"They weren't Indians, Pope," Matt said gently.

"You keep saying that, Marshal, but . . ."

"They were two of Ned Honeyman's riders, Earl Brant and Joe Carter."

Pope stared at him for a moment. "You know this for a fact?" When Matt nodded, he went on: "Well, then, what was their game?"

Matt ignored the question. "One of them, Joe Carter, stopped one of your bullets. He's dead."

Harry Pope went very pale. "Marshal! Are you sure?"

"Brant took Carter's body back to the ranch," Matt went on. "It looks like you've made a serious mistake, Pope."

He gripped one hand with the other. "Then I—you say I've killed a man, this fellow Carter?"

"It looks that way. Tell me, Pope—has there been any trouble between you and these two men?"

"Why, no! I hardly know them. I've seen them in town, and they've ridden by here a few times. Marshal, I wouldn't have shot at them if I'd known who they were!" He paused, considering. "But how *could* it have been them? *They were shooting at the house!* Why would they have done that? It doesn't make sense . . ."

"Look," Matt said patiently. "You say you've been hearing Indians around your place here. Well, Indians don't act that way. But you *think* you've heard 'em. It's got worse and worse, and so the other night when you heard these men ride by you got panicky and started shooting."

"I wasn't panicky," Pope protested. "I was just fed up."

"Well, whatever," Matt conceded, "I don't figure you aimed to kill Carter."

"Then . . . you're not going to arrest me?" the homesteader faltered.

"No, I'm not," Matt said. "Not until I get the straight of the thing, anyway."

"Maybe we oughta talk to Earl Brant, Marshal," Chester put in.

"All right, Chester," Matt said, "but we'll just let him come to us, I think. He'll come. Him and Honeyman too." He turned to Harry Pope. "Now don't go trying to make a run for it," he warned. "You wouldn't get very far."

"I know that, Marshal," Pope said fervently. "And I won't." He followed them outside. "I'm not . . . a murderer, Mr. Dillon. You know that."

They left him standing dejectedly beside his sodhouse. Matt waved a farewell to him but he didn't seem to notice. He was probably wishing now that he'd never left Boston, Matt thought.

When they were beyond earshot, Chester said, "I'm sure sorry for that there tenderfoot. Even if he is loco."

"Well, Chester, I'm not at all sure he's loco. I expect Earl Brant knows something he hasn't told Ned Honeyman." He gigged his horse into a faster pace. "Anyway, we'll soon find out."

Ned Honeyman showed up in Matt's office the following morning. He had a tall, towheaded, moonfaced cowboy with him.

"Morning, Marshal," the rancher said. "You know Earl Brant, been workin' for me for some time."

"I know him, Ned." Matt nodded at the cowboy. "How are you, Brant?"

Brant muttered that he was able to stick on a horse. He kept his face screwed into a frown, giving the impression that he was trying to look tough, Matt thought.

"Figgered you'd want to hear Earl's report of what happened at Pope's place the other night." Honeyman didn't wait for Matt's approval. "Go ahead, Earl."

"Well, me and Joe Carter was good friends," Brant announced. "I don't aim to rest till that Yank sodbuster's hung."

"I'm listening," Matt responded. "Tell me about it."

"Well, there really ain't much to it. Me and Joe was ridin' past his place, and the bustard come out and started whangin' away at us. He knocked Joe outa the saddle and so I threw some lead at him and chased him back inta that hut of his, and then I packed Joe back to the ranch."

The cowboy finished, eyeing Matt belligerently. The marshal got out his Durham and wheat straws.

"You'll swear to that in court, I suppose, Brant?" he asked.

"Sure he will!" Honeyman interjected.

"Now why wouldn't I, Marshal?" Brant demanded. "That snotty little killer been tellin' you somethin' different?"

"Well, yes," Matt said. "Harry Pope thought he was defending himself against Indians."

"*What?*" Honeyman roared, incredulous. "Why, that miserable son . . ."

"Ned, you weren't there," Matt pointed out. "How do you know what really happened?"

"Earl here told me, that's how!" snapped the rancher.

Matt faced the cowboy. "Tell me, Brant—*why* do you think Harry Pope shot at you?"

"It happened right there at his place!" Brant blustered.

"I mean, what was his reason for shooting at you?" Matt persisted.

"Heck, I dunno, Marshal. He's loco, I guess. What difference does it make, anyhow? He killed Joe Carter."

"The difference between murder and something else, that's all," Matt shot back.

"Why don't you bring him out of his cell and ask him?" Honeyman said stridently. "If the fool tries any of his lies, I'll beat the truth out of him, I sure will!"

"I'll overlook that last," Matt told him, "except to say nobody abuses a prisoner of mine while I'm around. The fact is, though, Ned, Pope's not here." He spread his hands on the desk top. "He's not here because I didn't arrest him. I didn't arrest him because he told me he thought he was shooting at Indians—and I believed him."

Honeyman glared at him, his face mottled with heavy red. "For Pete's sake, it looks like you're the one's loco!"

"You mean you ain't goin' to arrest him at all?" Earl Brant put in. He didn't seem too sure of himself now, Matt thought, as the cowboy refused to meet his gaze, instead looking expectantly at his employer.

"I'm not going to make *any* arrest till I've found out what this was all about," Matt said.

"Well, I've told you what it's all about!" Brant said irascibly. He started for the door. "Come on, boss, let's get outa here; we're wastin' our time."

The rancher lingered. "Marshal," he said harshly, "no man kills a rider of mine and gets out of it by claiming he thought he was shooting Indians. You hear that? You think I'd *let* anybody get by with that?"

Brant turned back from the door, seemingly emboldened by his boss's stand. "Joe Carter was my friend, too," he supported.

"If the law won't see justice done, we will." The rancher's voice was heavy, his tones measured.

"I'll have to warn you, Ned," Matt said, matching Honeyman's grave accents. "If you try to take the law in your own hands, I'll arrest *you*."

Honeyman leaned his weight on the desk, propping himself on his huge fists. "Dillon, I always rated you a good man. Always respected you. Up to this morning. But *now* . . ." He paused, significantly.

Matt looked at the cowboy. "Brant, I'm inviting you to tell the truth," he said. "Whatever it is—tell it."

Brant moved toward the door again. "Ah, come on, Ned, like I told you, we're wastin' our time. This hombre's a tenderfoot-lover!"

Matt stopped him with a pointed-finger gesture. "All right, then—I'll tell you what I think. I think you and Joe Carter were fooling that poor devil . . . making him think there were Indians prowling around. I don't know why you were doing it: trying to drive him out of the country, maybe?"

Brant was sweating but he wasn't giving up. "Marshal, you sound more loco all the time!" He opened the door, said, "I'm leavin', Ned," and stepped outside.

Honeyman did not move. "For the last time, Dillon," he grated, "are you aiming to do anything about the murder of Joe Carter?"

Matt stood up. His gaze locked with Ned Honeyman's. "It just wasn't murder, Ned. Can't you see that?"

"Joe Carter's dead," the rancher said with finality. "The bullet that killed him was fired by that lowdown pup, Harry Pope. That's all I need to know." He turned and called, "Wait for me, Earl!"

That afternoon Marshal Matt Dillon rode back out to Harry Pope's homestead. It was a nasty situation, and after Honeyman and Brant had left he'd sat at his desk thinking about it. Ned Honeyman was a bullheaded man, arrogantly sure of himself and his own rectitude. But he was also essentially an honest man, of that Matt was sure, and he'd been in the country long enough to have quite a stake in it. With Harry Pope, it was different. He was a newcomer, and an uneasy one; he didn't really belong in this land: he was born for an easier, softer existence. Now Matt sighed as he rode along. He wasn't happy about the conclusion he'd reached, but it was the only clear solution he could see. . . .

When he reached the place he found Pope busy hoeing the few rows of unpromising-looking corn he'd planted. The marshal ground-hitched his horse and walked over to Pope, who straightened up and looked at him hesitantly.

"Well, Marshal—changed your mind?"

"No," Matt said; "no, I haven't."

Pope looked his relief but he said nothing.

"I don't know what their reasons were," Matt went on, "but I'm satisfied that Joe Carter and Earl Brant were the 'Indians' you heard. Trying to throw a scare into you . . ."

"Well, Mr. Dillon, I'm sure that you know about Indians and their ways, and I don't see why you'd lie about it. So if you say it was Carter and that other fellow, it must have been."

"Well, then, can you think of any reason why they'd be doing it?" Matt asked him.

"No, I can't," Pope said slowly. "None at all."

"Brant and Ned Honeyman want me to arrest you, Pope," Matt said, searching his face.

"But you're not going to—and I thank you for that, Marshal," Pope said warmly.

"I don't have any reason to." Then Matt added: "They're threatening to take the thing into their own hands."

Pope looked frightened again. "But can't you stop them?"

"I could have them put under bond to keep the peace," Matt told him. "If they moved against you then, I could do something about it—but it might be a little late for you."

Pope's face was grave and pale as Matt continued.

"Maybe you won't like this idea, but I think the smart thing for you to do would be to pull stakes and go somewhere else. I know it's not your fault but you've got enemies now and—well, you'd be a lot safer in some other place."

Pope's face was still pale but now his jaw set. "No, Marshal," he said. "I'm not going to run away. Let them come. I'll fight it out with them."

It was foolish talk, coming from such a man, but there was a pride and a dignity in it, too, that Matt could not ignore. Apparently there was more to this greenhorn Easterner than he had reckoned.

"That would mean more bloodshed," he pursued. "Yours, likely."

"However, that isn't my fault—as you said yourself. And as I see it, a man has a right to defend himself." Harry Pope looked inches taller as he said it.

"Sure," Matt conceded. "But you won't have any peace.

You'll start jumping at shadows, always looking over your shoulder."

"Mr. Dillon," Pope said clearly, "I do not intend to leave."

Matt sighed. "Think it over, anyway."

"I have thought it over," Pope said calmly.

Matt looked at him for a minute, a scrawny specimen from Boston, Massachusetts, gripping the hoe handle as if it could give him strength, exuding a new and stubborn determination. Then he turned to his horse.

"Well, I've said all I can," he ended, looking down from the saddle. "I'm sorry about this, Pope."

"Thank you, Marshal," was the response. "I regret that I cannot take your advice. You're a good man, and I realize you mean well . . ."

Matt rode away with a clipped *"Adios."* He was getting sick of being called a "good man" by somebody who was defying him. First Honeyman, and then this fool sodbuster. He wished he could ditch it all and go fishing. But this Pope, now, maybe he'd do to take along, eventually. Had a lot of grit for a greenhorn . . .

He was half a mile or more away when he heard the shot behind him. Reining sharply around, he raced the horse back toward the homesteader's place. When he got there he found Harry Pope lying on his face between the corn rows, dead. There was a bullet hole in his back.

Matt had his gun out. There was a saddled horse standing near the soddy. Matt edged around the sad little structure. Earl Brant was standing by the pigpen, looking at the grunting porkers inside. As Matt watched Brant raised the gun he held in his right hand. Apparently he was going to end the pigs' existence too.

Matt stopped him. "Drop your gun, Brant. . . . All right, now turn around."

The cowboy faced him. "How long you been here, Marshal?" he said, his voice higher than normal.

"Long enough, Brant. I saw Pope—I mean I saw Pope's body."

"I shot the dang sodbuster," Brant said needlessly.

"In the back, too," Matt said in disgust. "You ought to be real proud of that."

"He killed a pard of mine!" Matt wondered if the man actually felt the justification that he put into his words.

"Harry Pope didn't know what he was doing," Matt said.

"What were you two trying to do to him, anyway—you and Carter?"

"We was just havin' a little fun, that's all."

"Fun?"

"Well, Joe and me'd have a drink or two and then we'd ride over and give him a few warwhoops. The little fool'd set there in his hut and shake. Why, one night I sneaked up to the door and I could hear him in there cryin'—*cryin'*, fer cripes sakes!" Pure contempt weighted his final words.

"That must have been a lot of fun," Matt said acidly.

"Next day we rode back," Brant went on, seeming to wring some satisfaction out of the memory of it, "and listened to him tell how the Injuns was after him . . . he wanted the Army to come out and run 'em off!"

"Yes," Matt said; "I know."

"We'd 'a' been all right if he hadn't went and got himself that gun." The simple-minded Brant was feeling a little sorry for himself now, Matt could tell.

"I told him to."

"You did! . . . Then durn it, Joe got killed account of you!"

"Your reasoning doesn't impress me much," Matt said. "Tell me, Brant, did you think you'd get away with this?"

"Shucks, I was goin' to leave the country. I been around here long enough to suit me. You'd never of caught me."

"Does Ned Honeyman know about this?" Matt demanded.

"He sure 'nough heard me say I aimed to git Pope."

"And he told you to go ahead?" Matt pressed.

"Well—he said he hoped somebody'd git him." Brant looked at Matt, suddenly sweating. "That makes it his fault, don't it?" His voice rose eagerly. "He kind of ordered me to do it, you see?"

"Shut up!" Matt ground out. "Get your horse . . . No, wait—first we'll do what we can about Pope. Then we'll ride for Dodge."

It was too late to teach Earl Brant anything, if it ever had been a possibility. Ned Honeyman was a different matter; he was cut from different cloth—a man, Matt judged, of some intelligence and character. He wanted to be sure that Honeyman understood what had really happened. Otherwise, Matt feared, the rancher would set about spreading the word against the marshal and the law, and there were plenty of men in Dodge who'd be ready to listen to him. He'd have to get to Honeyman early, or the big cattleman would be busy setting a fire that would be hard to get under control.

It was after dark when they reached town, but Matt kept off Front Street anyway and rode up to the jail from the rear. Chester was there, and Matt had him lock Brant in a cell, telling him briefly what had occurred. Then he ascertained from the deputy that Ned Honeyman was in town. He headed for the rancher's favorite hangout, the Alafraganza.

Honeyman was there, drinking in moody solitude at one end of the long bar. Matt went over to him.

"Howdy, Ned."

Honeyman looked at him fiercely. "What you want?"

"I want to talk to you."

The rancher deliberately turned his back.

Matt controlled his urge to grab the man's shoulder and pull him around. "I talked to Earl Brant," he said. "I got the whole story out of him." Honeyman maintained his stance and his silence, and Matt went on. "He said he and Joe Carter had been 'having fun' with Pope—hurrawing the man. Pretending they were Indians."

The big man turned on him wrathfully. "You told *him* that this morning!"

"He admits it's true."

"Even so, was that reason enough to kill a man?" he demanded.

"Pope was acting in self-defense—or thought he was. He didn't intend to kill Joe Carter. He wouldn't have shot if he'd known who it was. Carter brought it on himself."

"I don't believe it!"

In spite of Honeyman's vociferous avowal, Matt thought he could read uncertainty in the man's eyes. He pressed on: "Ned, you want law in this country, don't you?"

"Maybe that depends on who's enforcin' it," Honeyman countered, his voice harsh and unyielding.

"Ned, you're playing with words," Matt accused. "It's the law that counts, and you know it."

"Well, the law says you can't kill a man and go free, don't it?"

"The law says you can't *murder* a man," Matt corrected.

"So who decides which it is?" Honeyman jerked out.

"I'd like you to decide it this time, Ned," Matt said quietly.

"You mean that?" Honeyman said, pouncing.

"I do."

"All right, then—you go arrest Pope, see that he gets hung, like he should—that's how I decide it!"

"I can't," Matt said. He let him have it then: "Harry Pope is dead."

The big rancher was taken aback for a moment. His mouth came open but he said nothing.

"You wanted him killed," Matt went on inexorably. "He's been killed, Ned."

"What the devil do you mean?" the other said hoarsely.

"This morning you said you'd take justice in your own hands, didn't you?"

"Well, yes—I did, but . . ." Honeyman waved his hands in a negative gesture.

"So now Harry Pope is dead," Matt concluded.

"When—how do you know?" he demanded weakly.

"This afternoon he was out hoeing that miserable little patch of corn he had," Matt said. "He forgot to watch behind him. He got a bullet in his back." Honeyman's defenses were crumbling, but Matt showed him no mercy. "Is that how you wanted it, Ned? All Harry Pope had was a sod hut, a few pigs, that sorry patch of corn. He didn't have much sense about this country, it seemed like, but he might have learned. We laughed at him, but I think now he might have fooled all of us. He didn't get much help, Ned. Your riders scared him so that he'd cower in that soddy and cry, Earl Brant told me."

"Marshal, I—" Honeyman began. "I . . . Lord!"

"So he got a gun," Matt continued, "and one night when they came he went out to fight them. You know, Ned, that took a darned sight of courage, for a man like Harry Pope. He did it, though. That should have tipped me off to the kind of man he was, but today I went out there and told him he'd best clear out, leave his place and go somewhere else—that you and Earl Brant were threatening to give him trouble."

As Matt paused, Honeyman leaned forward a little. "Well, what'd he say?"

"He said he wouldn't do it. Harry Pope stood up like a man and said he'd stick there and fight. So he stayed," Matt went on wearily, "but he didn't get a chance to fight. After all, what would a man like Harry Pope know about protecting his back?"

Ned Honeyman's face was drained of color. "Brant?" he said in a low voice. "He did it?"

"Earl Brant shot him in the back," Matt said. "Pope had a hoe in his hands."

"Matt," the rancher said, "what can I say?"

"I arrested Brant. He's in jail. He'll be tried for murder."

"Lord," Honeyman breathed. "And I'm . . . as guilty as he is."

"Brant will try to pin it on you, Ned. And you might have stopped it . . . but you encouraged it. You were hollering for 'justice', Ned. Fast justice. Not the law kind."

Honeyman bowed his head. "I . . . didn't understand."

"You didn't take the time to, Ned. The law was too slow for you."

He raised his head and there were tears in his eyes. "I ain't at all proud of what's happened, Matt," he said.

"No," Matt said slowly; "and it is a shameful thing. Men like you could give this country strength—if they threw their strength behind the law, instead of bucking it, or going around it."

Honeyman's outstretched hand was fumbling, beseeching. "Would it help any—help the law, I mean—if I was to get up in court and take my share of the blame for this?"

"Yes, Ned," Matt said gently. "That would help. It would help a lot."

The law was young out here on the frontier. Sometimes Matt Dillon thought that the only time people wanted it was when it could be made to act the way they'd act themselves if there wasn't any law to do it for them. But it wouldn't work that way. If you were guilty of violating the law you were punished. If you were innocent, you were protected. People seemed to be reluctant to accept that. Until they did there wouldn't be much justice under law. Men like Harry Pope would go on dying no matter how many Earl Brants got hanged.

But with more men like Ned Honeyman seeing the light, there would be fewer needless deaths. . . . The law, in all its majesty, would be there, to punish the guilty, to protect the innocent.

GONE STRAIGHT

Matt Dillon was taking it easy in Doc Adams's office when Chester showed up and said there was a fellow in the marshal's office looking for Matt. He asked Chester who the man was.

"Wouldn't tell me. Close-mouthed cuss. Looks like he's had a long, hard ride, though. Official stuff, I'd say . . ."

Matt turned to Doc Adams. "See you later at supper, Doc? We can finish our talk then."

"I'll eat with you, don't worry," Doc said. "Want to tell you a few more of the facts of Life, son!"

Matt said so long and went out with Chester. The weary-looking man slumped on a chair in the marshal's office had a drooping roan mustache and faded blue eyes. He got to his feet when Matt and Chester entered.

"You Marshal Dillon?" he asked in a brittle voice.

"That's me," Matt said.

"Zach Parker." He extended a hand. "Special deputy for the New Mexico Stock Raisers' Association."

Matt shook. "You're a long way from home, Parker."

"My work often brings me far afield, Dillon. You've heard of the Association, of course?"

Matt said he had. He offered the makings to Parker and when the man refused, taking out a stogie instead, rolled a smoke for himself. Parker struck a match, lighted Matt's cigarette, then his own stogie. Matt watched him through the billowing smoke.

"What's on your mind, Parker?"

"Marshal, I have a warrant with me—for the arrest of Dane Shaw."

Matt searched his memory, came up with a blank. Chester said, "Never heard that name around here."

Parker reached a folded paper from an inside pocket. "Here it is, Marshal." He handed it to Matt.

Matt sat down at his desk, unfolded the document, looked at it idly. "Who issued this warrant?"

"Judge Blent . . . Santa Fe."

Matt inspected it more carefully. It seemed all in order.

It called for the arrest of one Dane Shaw; it bore the signature of Judge Blent, and an official seal.

"You intend to serve this warrant, Parker?"

"I'm not empowered to serve warrants, Marshal. It's up to you."

"Well," Matt said, "aside from the fact I don't know who or where Dane Shaw is, I'm not at all sure I have the authority to serve it either. After all, this was issued in New Mexico."

"You're a marshal, Dillon. Let's not stand on technicalities."

Matt looked at him. He didn't like the man's tone or his manner. He curbed an impulse to tell him so. After all, his job was the law, and it was true enough that on the frontier technicalities did not count as much as they did in more settled, stable communities.

"You have any idea where this Dane Shaw is supposed to be?"

"We have information that he may be in or near Tascosa," Parker responded.

"Tascosa!" Matt was frankly puzzled. "That's down in the Panhandle, mister. Out of my territory, by quite a bit."

"I was instructed to deliver this warrant to you," Parker said simply.

"Why don't they get an officer down around there to handle it?" Matt demanded.

"Marshal, we want this man taken alive. He's dangerous, and he would recognize any of the lawmen from New Mexico or around Tascosa with nerve enough to tackle him. He won't know you. We want to avoid bloodshed, if possible."

The man's tone was placatory now. Matt knitted his brows.

"What's Shaw wanted so bad for, anyhow?"

"On charges of rustling, banditry, assault to kill. But the big thing is he used to ride with Billy the Kid."

" 'Used to'?"

"Shaw quit Billy's gang two years ago. Quarreled with him, apparently. If we can get him back to New Mexico to face these indictments, we figure maybe we can persuade him to testify against the Kid. We want to pin a murder charge on the Kid, make it stick, see him swing. We've got to break the back of this rustling gang."

"Sounds like you're pretty sure you'll take the Kid," Matt said.

"We've got Pat Garrett working on that," Parker said.

Matt whistled. It looked as if they really meant business. "Suppose I locate Shaw and get the drop on him, deliver him to you. He still might not turn coyote on the Kid even to have you quash those indictments. Where'd that leave you?"

"We'd have him where he'd do us no harm, anyway," Parker said imperturbably. "He worries us some. He's a leader, like the Kid—probably why they couldn't go on working together—and the thought is he might get a new gang organized and come back. We've got enough trouble now."

Matt nodded. It made sense. Thousands of cattle were rustled yearly from Old John Chisum's Jingelbob spread alone. Other New Mexico ranchers were hard hit. "All right, Parker," he said. "You coming along to Tascosa with us?"

"Not me." His eyes shifted away from Matt. "Got business in Abilene. Ought to be back here in a week, ten days. I'll hope to find Shaw here in your custody when I return. I'll then take him to Santa Fe with me."

Matt grinned. "You're an optimistic cuss."

"You have quite a reputation, Marshal," Parker offered.

"Well, what does Dane Shaw look like?"

"Six feet, a hundred and eighty, black hair. About thirty-five years old. Pleasant talking, gives the impression of being easygoing."

"Not too much there," Matt said.

"He's supposed to have a knife scar across his ribs, left side."

"Think we could sneak up on him when he's takin' a bath, Mr. Dillon?" Chester asked innocently.

Matt's quick grin offset Parker's frown. The marshal stood up. "Hope you have a good trip to Abilene, Parker," he said. "If you don't find us here when you get back, you better not wait. If we bring Shaw in later we can telegraph to you and you can send somebody to get him."

"Thanks, Marshal," Parker said. He tossed away his stogie and extended his hand. "We appreciate your help." He turned to leave. "Luck to you," he said.

When he had gone Chester asked if he should see about getting their horses ready.

"Too long a piece, Chester," Matt said. "We better ride the stage. We can make it with one change, I think. If we need saddle horses when we get there we can hire some."

Tascosa was a small town on the Canadian River in the Texas Panhandle. Formerly a meeting place for Indian bands and *comanchero* traders, it currently had some excuse for existence as a cattle-trail town but Matt suspected that a good share of the place's revenue came from illicit activities. John Chisum sometimes trailed a herd this way to market, but hundreds of other head of Jinglebob stuff had gone through here hazed along by riders never hired by Old John. Rustlers and midnighters hung around here when they had money to spend. Their cash looked just as good as anyone else's to the few businessmen in town.

Matt had been through the place before but it was new to Chester. He looked around after they'd gotten off the stage, and remarked favorably on the trees that grew round-about. A couple of buildings looked new to Matt. Another one seemed to be under construction although no workmen were presently in sight.

"Don't look like it's goin' to be a house," Chester opined. "Or a store either. Not even a saloon."

"Might be a schoolhouse," Matt said; "but that I doubt. Not enough honest citizens around here to figure they need a school."

"No citizens at all, honest or not, I guess," Chester said, looking around at the empty street.

Matt headed for the bigger of the two new buildings. "Could be we can find out a few things in here."

Chester read the sign above the boardwalk. "The Red Deer—pretty fancy name for a saloon, ain't it?"

"Never judge a package by its wrapping, Chester. Let's withhold judgment till we sample their beer."

They pushed through the swing door. The saloon's interior was as empty as the street except for the man behind the bar. He was of middle height and slight in build. His face, Matt noted, was tanned and weathered, not pale like the average saloonkeeper's. He gave them his attention.

"What'll it be, gents?"

They asked for beer and he set it out. Chester drank thirstily. Matt took a swallow and put his glass on the bar top.

"Place has changed some," he commented.

"Yeah," the barman said. "Quite a lot, for a town this size. We're growin' up fast, you might say." He grinned at Matt.

"Building going up down the street looks like a school-house . . ."

"Which is what it is. Few family men have come in. Kids needed a school, so we got one started."

"No offense," Matt said, "but I didn't think there was anyone here with enough sense of civic responsibility to get anything like a school under way."

"Only one man around meetin' that description," the barkeep admitted. "My boss, Nat Timble."

"A saloonkeeper building a school?" Matt looked his surprise.

"Kind of unusual, I reckon. Guess you could call Nat Tascosa's leadin' citizen. I do, myself."

"You make him sound like quite a man," Matt said. "He around?"

"Out back," was the answer. "Buildin' a hitchrail. You want to talk to him, the door's right there."

"Thanks." Matt laid a coin on the bar. "We'll do that." He headed for the back entrance, Chester trailing behind.

"You're right, mister," the barkeep called after them. "Nat Timble's a real man."

As they emerged from the Red Deer the heavy-shouldered man who had been busy with hammer and nails glanced up. He laid down the tool and wiped the sweat from his face with a blue bandanna. He took a step toward them, then stopped.

"Looking for me?" It was pleasantly enough spoken but to Matt it sounded partly a challenge. He took stock of the man. He was all of six feet, Matt judged. The hair that showed under his broad-brimmed hat was black, streaked with a little gray. He was probably in his mid-thirties, but his weight was pushing closer to two hundred than one-eighty. A man of his build could put on that much fairly quickly, given easy living, Matt knew, and he wondered if this could be the man he held a warrant for. Chances were that it wasn't, though.

"You Mr. Timble?" Matt asked.

He nodded. "Nat Timble."

"Matt Dillon," the marshal said. "This is Chester Proudfoot."

"Nice to know you gents," Timble said. His eyes stayed on Matt. "Your name sounds familiar."

"U. S. Marshal," Matt said easily. "Dodge City."

He was watching the man. He thought the facial muscles

stiffened a tiny bit but he couldn't be sure. And when Timble spoke his tone was calm.

"A far piece. Must be here on business, Marshal."

"We are," Matt said. "Looking for a man named Dane Shaw . . ." He paused. Timble's eyes were steady. "You know him?"

"Can't say I do. Never heard of anyone around by that name, even."

"He's on the dodge," Matt said. "Might be running under an alias."

"Hard to tell, then," Timble observed. "No use denyin' there's enough men on the dodge around Tascosa, Marshal."

"Six foot, black hair," Matt went on. "Weighs a hundred and eighty."

"Fits a lot of men," Timble said. He chuckled. "Might fit me, even, was I fifteen, twenty pounds lighter."

"One other thing. He's got a scar across his ribs."

"You don't often see a feller without his shirt on, Marshal. If you down him, though, you can make sure that way —just pull out his shirt-tail." The big man grinned.

"I don't figure on shooting him, Trimble, if that's what you mean. He has to be brought in alive."

"Didn't go to offend you, Marshal. I've heard tell you're not kill-crazy. Well, I wish I could help you, but I dunno how I can. What's this feller—Shaw, you call him?—wanted for?"

"Grand theft, in New Mexico. Used to ride with Billy the Kid. I was told he's under indictment and if they can get him back there they aim to go light on him if he'll testify against the Kid—*if* they manage to get the Kid roped and tied."

Timble digested that briefly. "Sounds like one too many 'ifs' there—the one about the Kid, I mean."

"Pat Garrett is heading it up," Matt told him quietly.

"Pat Garrett?" Timble echoed. "Well, it'll still take a lot of doing . . . But it's none of my mix. Got enough troubles of our own around here. Take my barkeep, for instance— Mike Postil in there."

"Seemed decent enough to me," Matt said. "Spoke like you graded out high with him, too. What trouble's he giving you?"

Timble waved a hand. "Oh no, I don't mean it's Mike. *He's* the one that's got the trouble." He lowered his voice. "Mike used to run with a wild bunch. I don't mean there's any secret about it—and I know well enough he ain't the man you're lookin' for, from the description. Used to be top gun for Harry Gunter. You heard of Gunter?"

Matt shook his head and Timble went on. "Gunter owns a ranch a few miles out and he runs a puny little herd of ticky stuff. But he has seven or eight riders out there, all hardcases, and he trails a lot of New Mexico beef through here off and on. Everyone knows what he's up to, but it ain't been proved on him. He's been riding high and mighty, anyways up till lately, and that mainly because of Mike."

"How d'you mean?"

"Mike's fast with a gun. Fast as I've ever seen. When he was siding Harry Gunter, why nobody was about to brace Harry, and that's a fact."

"And now he tends bar for you . . . how come, Timble?"

"Mike got sick of the whole deal and decided he'd go straight. He told me one night he was quitting Gunter's bunch. Didn't want to hire out his gun any more, and thought he'd best pull stakes. I told him if he'd rather stay in Tascosa the bar job was his. I can't help feelin' for a man like that."

Timble's eyes had a faintly troubled look as he paused. Matt glanced at him sharply, and was about to speak but Timble went on.

"He'll make out all right, if Harry Gunter leaves him be. It's tough enough to break off like that and try to live an honest life when they leave you alone . . ."

"You deserve a lot of credit for giving the man a hand," Matt observed; "but why're you telling me all this, Timble?"

The saloon owner looked at him, his face serious. "I was thinkin' about this other guy, Marshal—the one you're lookin' for. If he quit the Kid's gang two years back, like you say, and ain't been heard of since, could be he's tryin' to make a new start, an honest one, somewheres. If he did, I hope nobody gets to rawhidin' him, and forces him back across the line."

"It's an interesting point," Matt said, "but it all sounds pretty blue-sky to me. It isn't often that an outlaw suddenly decides to turn honest, and then does it. If Mike Postil has done it and can make it stick, more power to him, I say. But I'm more interested in this Harry Gunter. If Shaw is living around Tascosa, it could be he's riding with Gunter's bunch. Do you know the men in it?"

"Most of 'em I've seen, anyway," Timble answered. "But the man who can tell you all you want to know about that is Mike Postil. Let's talk to him."

The three of them went back into the Red Deer. Matt questioned the bartender. Postil shot an anxious glance at his employer when he realized that Matt was a lawman but Timble assured him that Matt's sole interest was in locating a man named Dane Shaw. Postil had never heard the name, he said at first; under Matt's prodding he said he recalled hearing at one time that Billy the Kid was being sided by a man named Shaw. He hadn't heard the first name. No, Shaw had never shown up in Tascosa, to his knowledge. Neither had there ever been a member of Gunter's outfit answering the description which Matt gave him.

At the end of the session, Matt felt he and Chester needed a meal. Timble asked them to come to his house for supper but Matt thought they shouldn't put Timble's wife to the bother. Talkative over a beer, Timble told Matt and Chester that he'd brought his bride here right after their marriage, and she was well and happy here, although she'd always lived in Dallas. They were both raised in east Texas, he said; he himself had spent several years in Colorado after serving almost four years in the Confederate Army.

Finally Timble left to go home and eat. Matt assured him they'd be around for some time and could take a meal with him and his wife later. The saloonkeeper had advised them to get their food at the Star, calling it the one decent eating place in the town. Matt and his deputy went there and had a long and leisurely meal. Tascosa's best proved to be none too good. Everything was overcooked but it was filling and the coffee was not bad. At the end of the meal Matt sighed, stretched back in his chair and rolled a cigarette.

"You think we'll locate this here Dane Shaw ever?" Chester asked him plaintively. "Don't seem like we got anywhere a-tall today."

Matt glanced around. No one was near them. He looked back at his deputy. "Now you ask me, Chester," he said, "I think we've found him already."

Chester was thunderstruck. "Why, that bartender cain't be him!" he said. "He don't fit the description one bit."

"I don't mean Mike Postil," Matt said.

Chester looked blank, then thoughtful, then doubtful. "Well, now . . . sure, he does look about like Shaw's supposed to . . . said as much himself . . . except he's too heavy . . . like he said, too . . ." The deputy narrowed his eyes, wagged his head.

Matt said, "It's not just the appearance, Chester. Timble knew that Dane Shaw quit the Kid two years ago: he thought I'd mentioned that but I hadn't. Bringing up this business about Postil going straight and comparing it to the possibility of Shaw's doing the same thing—pretty farfetched unless it was mighty close to home. Giving me all his back history when I hadn't asked for it . . ."

"Well, he does seem like a natural-born talker, Marshal," Chester pointed out.

"He does, at that," Matt admitted. He closed his eyes a moment. "Still, it all adds up. He breaks up with Billy the Kid, comes here not to recruit a new gang but to start new under another name. He probably went to Dallas first to marry this girl he'd known there before. Why he'd bring her here to settle down I don't know . . . maybe somebody back in east Texas knew about his record . . . but here he wasn't known by sight, and the law is conspicuous mostly by its absence. Things go good for him. Then this Postil business comes up, and out of a natural sympathy for another ex-outlaw trying to walk the straight-and-narrow he goes out of his way to help him."

Finished, Matt stayed silent for a moment. Chester stirred.

"Well, if he's him, are you goin' to arrest him, Marshal—or ain't you just sure enough, 'spite of all that brainy talk?"

"Let's wait awhile, Chester," Matt said. "Not because I'm not sure, for I am—sure enough to risk an arrest, anyway—but because I'm not sure if I *want* to arrest Dane Shaw."

Chester stared at him. "Look, Marshal, we come here to—"

Matt waved him quiet. "Sure we did. But I don't know how much good it would do. If this man has guts enough to turn his back on his past, go straight and stay that way, and help another man in the same kind of trouble, I doubt like heck if he'd go State's evidence against a man he'd ridden with just to save his own hide."

"But Parker said they wanted him anyway, whether he'd coyote on the Kid or not," Chester reminded him.

"Sure—because they were afraid he might go back there with a bunch of his own, don't forget. It doesn't look to me like he's getting ready to do anything like that. Why, he's got a *settled* look: getting fat and happy . . . or was until we came along."

"We lettin' him *stay* happy, then?"

"We're letting things ride for awhile, let's say." Matt stood up. "If you've had enough pie let's go."

They went out. Dusk had fallen while they were eating and it was difficult to make out the far end of the town's short street. Lights shone in the Red Deer and a few other places. Off-key piano music and a woman's shrill laughter emerged from one building. The music stopped but the high-pitched laughter went right on. Then it too ceased, at a hoarsely shouted obscenity.

Matt and Chester ambled in the direction of the Red Deer, enjoying the light breeze which had developed after sundown. They were close to the saloon when a group of horsemen rode in swiftly from the south. Matt counted seven of them. They pulled up before the Red Deer and went in. As they did so one of them shot a low-voiced query at the man who seemed to be leading them, calling him "Harry." This man snapped back, "He'll be here!"

Chester was remarking that they were a mean-looking bunch when Matt snapped away his half-smoked cigarette, touched the deputy on the arm and hurried toward the front door. Once in, Matt led the way to a small table. He sat down with his back to the wall and put his attention on the group at the bar. Chester followed suit.

The men standing there were clustered about the one Matt had heard addressed as "Harry." He was directing some comment to Mike Postil, but in such a low voice that Matt could not distinguish the words. Postil was leaning forward to listen. Then he went erect. His lips moved in speech and Matt guessed he was asking them what they would have. The leader crashed his fist on the bar top. In the silence that followed he said:

"We didn't come here to drink, durn it!"

"This is a saloon, gents," Postil said calmly.

"And I've seen better ones in the middle of the desert!" the other retorted. "Never mind that. Postil, you're the first man ever walked out on me and I ain't going to stand for it!"

"I don't see what you can do about it, Harry," Postil said reasonably.

"I need your gun," said the man who Matt was now sure was Harry Gunter.

"I'm all through sellin' my gun," Postil answered simply.

"That wouldn't be so bad, maybe," Gunter snarled, "but you know too darn much about my business!"

"Harry, you know me better'n that. I'm not goin' to talk about your business."

Strangely, the assurance seemed to enrage Gunter. He gripped the edge of the bar. "Sure you won't!" he fairly screamed at the bartender. "You won't because you're coming back to work for me!"

Postil took off his apron. Matt knew from seeing him earlier that he carried a gun in a leather-lined pocket-holster sewed to the right leg of his trousers. "I'd like to know which one of you's goin' to bring me back," he said.

Gunter pushed back from the bar. Hatred blazed from him. He made an apparent effort to control himself.

"I'm giving you forty-eight hours," he said. "I want you back at the place by dusk day after tomorrow. If you don't show I'll ride in for you—with the boys. They're all with me on this—they figure we can't afford to have you running loose. Right, boys?"

There was a growling chorus of assent. Mike Postil looked at them with no sign of concern. "The answer'll be the same then as now. You know me, all of you. You come after me shootin', I'll take some of you with me."

"You can't handle the whole bunch of us," Gunter rapped. "So think it over." He turned on his heel and started away.

It was Nat Timble's voice that stopped him. The big man had come out of his office room in the rear halfway through the argument and had given it his quiet attention. Now he stepped forward.

"Now wait a minute, Gunter," he called.

Harry Gunter stopped and turned. "What d'*you* want, Timble? Seems to me you've made enough trouble already."

"I'll tell you this—if you come back here again after Mike Postil it won't be just him you'll be facing. I'm dealing myself in on it."

"No, now, Nat," Postil began; "I won't—"

"Shut up, Mike," Timble said without looking at him. "You heard me, didn't you, Gunter? Count on me being here, too."

"So suit yourself then," Harry Gunter ground out. "If

you choose to be a fool I can't help it. *You hear me*: we're coming after Postil if he don't show up. If you're here in the way, we'll give you the same medicine we aim for him to get. Come on, boys."

On the way out his hot-eyed stare swept over Matt and Chester. He paused in mid-stride, gave them a flashing scrutiny, then proceeded to the door. His men tramped out after him.

Matt went to the bar as Chester peered over the top of the swing door to watch them leave.

"Well, Marshal," Nat Timble said, "you've seen Harry Gunter in action."

"So I gathered," Matt said. "He talks mighty big."

"Ain't all talk, either," Mike Postil said, tying his apron back on. "He's always been mean, and he keeps gettin' worse. He don't need me *that* bad, and he knows darn well I won't talk. He just can't stand the idea of me quittin' him— messes up the big picture of himself he's got in his head, I reckon . . . He'll be back, all right—with the others."

"We'll face them down, Mike," Timble told him.

"*I* will, Nat—this ain't your nest o' snakes."

"I helped you get into this, Mike," Timble told him quietly. "And I'll see you through it."

"It ain't your fight, I say!" Postil sounded exasperated.

Timble stood firm. "It is my fight. Any man willing to make the jump you're making deserves all the backing he can get. Am I right, Marshal?" he appealed to Matt.

"In a way, you are," Matt conceded. "I have to stay clear of it, though. It's not my job to keep the peace in Tascosa. I'm only here to serve a warrant on a man I haven't found yet. But I wish you luck. Both of you."

"Well, I didn't figure you *could* mix in here, Marshal. All I wanted was an expression of opinion."

Postil wouldn't give up. He turned back to his employer. "You got no call to do it, Nat. You're a married man."

"Nothing to do with the case," Timble announced. "We can't give in to a thing like this, anyway. Bad for the town." Frowning, he said seriously, "Mike, I never told you going straight'd be easy."

"Heck, you shoulda been a preacher." Postil untied his apron again. "I got to go eat. See you in a little while."

Timble watched him go, compassion in his face. Then he turned to Matt and chuckled. "Me a preacher!" he said.

"Well, if business don't pick up I might give it a whirl at that."

"Town's growing," Matt said. "You ought to do all right."

"Yeah," Timble responded, "it is, at that. Quite a bit, even since I been here."

Matt pulled out the makings. "How long did you say that was, Timble—that you've been here?"

"Almost two years," he said. "A year and nine months . . ." His eyes widened. He reached over the bar for a bottle of whisky. "Whew," he said; "thing like that calls for a drink."

Forty-eight hours passed. At deadline time, Mike Postil was calmly serving drinks behind the bar of the Red Deer. He saw Matt watching him and paused long enough to give him a wink and a grin. Matt glanced at Timble. The saloon owner's expression was drawn and grim.

The next morning, early, Matt and Chester rode south from town. A couple of miles out, they pulled their horses off the trail and concealed themselves in a scrub-cedar thicket. Chester seemed preoccupied and at last he said querulously:

"Marshal, I thought you said the other night that it wasn't our job to keep the peace in Tascosa and we had to stay clear of all this?"

"Chester," Matt said gravely, "a great man once said that consistency is the hobgoblin of little minds."

"Well, yes," Chester said, "but what about what I said?"

"Listen. I've had plenty chance to talk to this Nat Timble, and watch him. I'm satisfied he's Dane Shaw, all right. So we may have to take him back to Dodge with us. But I'm also satisfied he's straight as an arrow now, no matter what he was once. Not only that but he's risking his neck to help Mike Postil, which he doesn't have to do."

"Yeah," Chester said. "And you talked to Mrs. Timble —or Shaw, whatever her name really is—about him too, didn't you?"

"I did, Chester. She impressed me as being a good woman, as I reckon she did you too." Chester nodded. "She told me her husband was the finest man alive, and I could see she believed it through and through. You don't get the respect and admiration of a woman like that unless you've got quite a lot of good in you, Chester. Love, maybe, but not respect and admiration."

"Guess you're right, Marshal." Chester sat erect in the saddle. "And yonder they come."

Matt, looking, saw a group of horsemen riding north toward them. They were coming at a good pace, riding purposefully. One man was in the lead; the others followed him in twos. Matt counted three pairs following the leader. Seven men. Gunter's bunch, riding to Tascosa. Coming after Mike Postil. . . .

"That's them, all right," Chester said.

"You don't have to do this, Chester," Matt told him.

"You object to me usin' a rifle?" the deputy said.

"There's no rules in this game, Chester," Matt said bleakly.

Chester pulled his rifle out of the saddle boot. "Always feel a mite cozier behind a Winchester," he announced.

Matt drew his Colt's, checked the loads, eased it back into the holster. He let the horsemen come on. When he thought they were close enough he said, "All right, Chester." They pulled out of the thicket onto the trail. The oncoming riders saw them and slowed to a stop. Their horses milled around. Gunter alone came toward them.

"Hold it, Gunter," Matt called.

"What is this?" Gunter said harshly. "Who are you?"

"U. S. Marshal," Matt said. "Dillon's my name; Matt Dillon."

"Them two was there the other night, Harry," a burly, whiskered rider called. "At Timble's saloon."

"All right," Gunter said. "Clear the trail, you. I don't give a hoot if you're a U. S. Senator. You've got no business with us. Clear the trail, I said!"

"Turn around and ride south, Gunter. Back where you came from. Mike Postil's staying in Tascosa."

"So that's it!" Blood rushed to Harry Gunter's face. "What're you doing in this game?"

"I dealt myself in, Gunter. Now do as I say. Clear out. Keep away from Tascosa from now on. Leave Mike Postil alone. Leave Nat Timble alone. Leave the town alone. Fade away. Do you get that?"

Gunter's eyes widened so that Matt could see white all around them. The man was gripped by fury.

"We don't need any lawmen down here, Dillon!" he shouted. "Why don't you line out for wherever you came from? That'd be the smart thing for you to do!"

Matt heard horses coming from the north, behind him. "Who's that, Chester?" he called sharply.

"Mike Postil, and Mr. Timble," Chester answered.

"Well, Marshal," Gunter said in savage triumph, "it looks like we won't have to go into Tascosa! We can settle things right here!"

The saloon owner rode up beside Matt. "Missed you this morning," he said. "Thought you might be down this way."

Mike Postil grumbled, "Durn it, Marshal. First Nat, an' now you. This is *my* trouble."

Matt ignored him. "Well, Gunter," he said, "the odds are considerably lower than they were."

"They sure are," the whiskered man in Gunter's bunch said loudly. "The heck with this. I'm gettin' out. Come on, Harry; we kin fix Postil's wagon later. When there ain't such a crowd, maybe."

"Stand by me, dang it!" Gunter rasped at the man.

"You heard me," the other said. "I'm goin'."

"I said stand!" Gunter, his face livid, spurred his mount toward Nat Timble's. "You rat, you're to blame for this!" he shouted.

"Keep back!" Timble cried at him. "No closer, I say!"

Gunter kept his horse coming. He grabbed his gun, pulled it out. "Get him first," he yelled at his men, "then Postil!"

"Drop that, Gunter!" Matt yelled at him. His own Colt's was out.

Gunter fired at Timble at point-blank range. The saloon owner, trying to draw his own gun, tipped from the saddle. Matt dropped to the ground for accuracy's sake, holding his horse's reins with his left hand. He aimed and fired at Gunter, who was trying vainly to get a bead on Postil as his horse plunged wildly. Postil's own animal reared, and the bartender left saddle, let it go, and began firing calmly. Chester was working his Winchester, astride his horse. Some of Gunter's riders had broken and run when the fight started, but a couple, either desperate or suddenly battle-happy, were throwing lead promiscuously.

It couldn't have lasted more than four or five minutes. To Matt, later, it seemed like an hour. He had plenty of time to empty his Colt's, firing carefully at targets. Timble was stretched on the ground, not moving. Gunter lay in a huddled heap, and the two of his men who had stayed to fight were lying near by, one silent, the other breathing in gasps and bubbling moans.

"Shall we chase the others?" Chester was saying.

"Never mind them," Matt said. "Timble's down, we'd better help him." He walked over to the still form. "Look at Gunter and the others, Chester," he said.

Postil came up as he knelt beside Timble. "How is he, Marshal?"

"Shot in the head," Matt said.

"I told him not to come," Postil said. "We better get him back to his house."

"No use," Matt said. "He's gone. Probably before he hit the ground."

Postil cursed.

"I'm sorry, Mike."

"He'd done enough for me already," Postil said. "Why'd he have to do this? It was my fight, not his."

"Not the way he looked at it, Mike. He went straight himself a while back. He knew what a job it was."

Postil looked from Matt to the dead man and back. "You sure?"

"I came down here with a warrant to arrest him, Mike."

"He was . . . Dane Shaw?"

"Dane Shaw had a knife scar on his ribs," Matt said. "Right side."

Slowly, Mike Postil loosened the shirt, pulled it open. He had his look. "Yeah," he said. "He was Dane Shaw, all right."

Chester came over to them. "Those three are all done for," he said to Matt. "Gunter and the little guy are goners already. The other one's got a few minutes. I made him as comfortable as I could."

Postil was staring at Matt. "I can't figger you—comin' here to arrest him, then sidin' him and me against Harry Gunter and his bunch."

"Don't try," Matt told him. "Just try to remember what kind of a man Nat Timble was."

"He was one really good man, Marshal," Postil said fervently.

Matt turned to Chester. "You stay here with Mike. I'll send a wagon out from town. I've got to tell his wife."

Nora Timble turned her face and wept bitterly when Matt

told her what had happened. He had her sit down and waited quietly till she could look at him, her steady blue eyes glistening.

"You . . . tried to stop it," she said. "Thank you for that."

"My job," he said. "What are you going to do, Mrs. Timble?"

"I may go back to Dallas," she said. "I don't know. Anyway, Mike Postil will have to . . . run things now."

"Mike's all right," Matt said. "He'll make out."

"Tell me . . . one thing, Marshal," she went on.

"What is it, Mrs. Timble?"

"Did you come here . . . to arrest my husband?"

He gauged her with a look. She had the basic strength. She knew, somehow, anyway . . . "Yes," he said. "I did."

"He'd told me what was behind him," she said quietly. "I figured he had."

"If this thing today hadn't happened . . . would you have taken him back?"

He waited a moment. "I can't tell you, Mrs. Timble. Because I don't know . . . But if I had, it would've been my last official act."

"You mean you would have quit afterward?" she asked softly.

"Yes," he said.

"Marshal," she said, extending her hand, "if you come back to Tascosa, please call."

"It would be a pleasure, Mrs. Timble," Matt Dillon said.

JAYHAWKERS

The first big herd to come up the trail to Dodge in the spring of '77 was bossed by a big burly Texan named Dolph Quince. He had brought a herd up the year before, so Matt knew him, liked him in a way. He'd had to buffalo a couple of Quince's riders who were bent on taking the town apart but although the big Texan didn't like seeing his men manhandled he'd had sense enough to realize Matt was only doing his job and hadn't tried to interfere.

This year Quince was bringing a larger herd than the year before, three thousand head. Most of them were destined for the Dodge City shipping pens, but five hundred selected stockers had to be trailed through clear to Ogallala for one of the new ranches being set up on the northern range.

Matt knew none of these things the day he and Chester were taking it easy in front of the marshal's office. It was a soft spring day and, keenly aware of the fact that their slack season was about over, they were making the most of it.

"Man," Chester breathed, "have I got spring fever . . ."

"Well, get it out of your system," Matt said; "first trail herd'll hit us before long."

"I wish you hadn't brought that up, Marshal," Chester said. "Them Texas cowboys, they're a trial."

"Oh, they're not so bad, Chester," Matt said tolerantly.

"They're just born troublemakers!" the deputy said sternly. "At home, they're bad enough. They're worse, away from it."

Matt grinned. "Where's it you hail from, now?"

"Well, Waco," Chester said. "But that don't make no never-mind! Just shows I know what I'm talkin' about."

"I see your point, Chester, I see your point," Matt said soothingly. He turned his head to look down the street. A rider was coming toward them. His horse looked nearly played out, but the man wasn't letting him ease along. Matt straightened up.

"Looks like one of your Texans coming now," he said to Chester. "Rim-fire hull," he noted, meaning the double-rigged saddle which the trail drivers favored.

71

Chester looked. "Yeah," he said; "sure is. What you suppose he's doin' here?"

"Looking for someone to shoot up, according to you," Matt said drily. He watched as the rider slowed his mount and reined up, looking toward them. "Don't know the fella, do you, Chester?"

"Well, no," the deputy said; "but I suppose practically everybody I used to know in Texas has been hung by now," he added, poker-faced.

Matt grinned. The newcomer stepped down from his saddle and bowlegged over to them. He looked weary and worried.

"I'm lookin' for the marshal, and you're wearin' a star," he said to Matt. He was a towheaded youngster with a good, square-jawed face.

"You've come to the right place, stranger," Matt told him.

He seemed to need more confirmation than that. "You Matt Dillon?"

"That's my name."

"Good." He relaxed. "Mine's Phil Jacks. I'm with a herd 'bout five days' drive down the line yet. Dolph Quince sent me up ahead, he's my boss."

"Dolph was here last year," Matt said. "We got along fine. Give him my regards when you see him."

"You give 'em to him, Marshal," Jacks said, heel-squatting and pulling out his sack of Durham.

Matt glanced at him, puzzled. Was the man quitting his outfit, before the herd was even delivered? "All right," he said noncommittally. "He'll be here in about five days, you say?"

"Yeah," said Jacks, twisting up his smoke, "if he don't run into no more trouble." He lighted up and took a deep drag. "He told me to ask you to ride back to the herd with me, Marshal."

Matt was silent for a moment. He looked at Chester. The deputy was watching the Texan, his eyes wide.

"Can you tell me what this is all about?" Matt finally asked.

"Well, Dolph didn't spell it out none," was the Texan's rejoinder. "But I reckon it's about Kansas."

"Kansas?" Matt echoed. "What d'you mean?"

"Well sir, we just don't like it."

Matt smiled but to his surprise Chester burst out: "Then

why don't you fellas stay in Texas instead of comin' up here, raisin' the devil, drinkin' and shootin' and . . ."

"Whoa up there, boy!" Matt halted him. "What's got into you?"

Before the deputy could respond, Jacks said, grinning at Chester, "I know what's the matter of him, he's from Texas hisself and he's all riled up 'cause he don't like Kansas any better'n nobody else does."

To Matt's relief, Chester grinned back at the trailsman. "How'd you know I was from Texas?"

"Know a Texan when I see one, I should hope," Jacks said easily. He turned to Matt. "Can you go, Marshal?"

"Well," Matt replied, "Dolph Quince is all right; I don't suppose he'd've sent you for me without a pretty good reason."

"He'll sure appreciate it, Marshal," Jacks said.

Matt looked at Chester. "You better take Jacks over to the Dodge House for a good feed, he looks like he could use it. I'll get ready and meet you over there in an hour."

"Don't you want me to go?" Chester asked.

"Well, it'll likely be quiet till those uncombed Texans of yours hit town, but maybe you better stay anyway," Matt said.

"All right." Chester turned to the Texan. "Come on with me, Phil, it's just down the street."

"I'll see that your horse gets put away, Phil," Matt said as the pair started off. "We'll rustle you up a fresh one to ride back."

"Thanks, Marshal," Jacks said over his shoulder.

"Now don't shoot him, Chester," Matt called to his deputy; "I'll need him to guide me to Dolph's herd."

Phil Jacks laughed. "I aim to buy him a drink first, and calm him down."

"Well that ain't a bad idea," Matt heard Chester saying, and they were gone.

Matt Dillon had not been out on the prairie for several weeks. He found himself enjoying the ride. Its customary monotony was broken by the great patches of fresh green growth which stood out in contrast to the dun of last year's grass. The sun was bright, the air was caressingly velvet on the skin; it was good to be alive. He let his mind reach back to the carefree days of his boyhood, when to ride a bronc somewhere meant heading for fun rather than going to face some unknown trouble.

He questioned Phil Jacks. It seemed that Quince's herd had encountered little but trouble since they had crossed the Washita. Man-made trouble, most of it. They had expected some, and were ready for it, but it kept getting worse, especially when they were nearly across the Indian Territory and nearing the Kansas line. Finally Quince had sent Phil Jacks larruping north to get Matt's help if he could. He was a close-mouthed cuss and didn't spill everything he thought but he'd seemed awful edgy about things. Phil thought he must have a lot of his own money tied up in the herd.

They kept a good pace and covered plenty of distance. They could have stopped at a stream with good water late in the afternoon but Matt preferred to keep going as long as they had light. At dark they made dry camp, ate quickly, and rolled into their blankets. They were in the saddle again at dawn. Phil Jacks thought they might run into his outfit by nightfall. Matt ventured to doubt it but Phil asserted that Quince was really "pushin' 'em."

His optimism proved well founded. They spotted trail dust ahead of them late in the afternoon. By the time they rode up to the chuck wagon most of the men had already eaten and the coozie was dishing up some chow for himself.

"Drop your saddle anywheres, Marshal," the tired towhead said; "I'll turn your horse in with the remuda."

Matt thanked him and looked around for Dolph Quince. He saw the tall Texan squatting near the fire with a tin plate of grub. He ambled over, acknowledging a couple of howdies from riders too beat out with fatigue to register more than scant curiosity.

Dolph Quince noticed him approaching, took a last hurried mouthful, put down his plate and stood up.

"Hello, Dolph," Matt greeted.

"Glad to see you, Marshal," the Texan responded.

They shook hands. Quince looked older than Matt recalled him, his face lined with worry and care.

"Fresh meat in camp," Quince said. "Have the cook give you a plate."

"Sounds fine," Matt said and started to head back for the wagon.

"I'll go along with you," the drover said; "need some more coffee. You like buffalo veal?"

"Sure do," Matt said. "Don't get it too often any more."

"One of the boys shot a calf this mornin' . . . maybe it was buffs that scared our hosses last night. Whole remuda busted loose."

"You don't make it sound like you really believed that, Dolph," Matt offered.

"Well, I don't." They were at the wagon. "Give this fella a plate o' that stuff, Coozie," Quince said to the cook.

The oldster with the tobacco-stained mustache ladled out a plateful and handed it to the marshal. Matt took it with a murmured thanks.

"Don't worry, Marshal," Quince told him; "he takes out his quid when's he's cookin'."

"Take it out, nothin'," the old man scoffed. "I swaller it. Ain't enough juice left t' say after I've worked on 'er all day, anyhow."

"I used to know a man that dried it out and smoked it after he got through chewing it," Matt said, winking at Dolph.

"Prob'ly one of them chinchy durn Yankees," the cook shot back. "I ain't that hard up, by Godfreys!"

Matt laughed and Dolph Quince joined in. They sat down and Matt pitched into his food while Quince sipped at his hot coffee.

"This is mighty good, Dolph," Matt said. "First eats I've had since morning."

"Lot of hungry folks around here," Quince remarked. "Nester woman come around early this mornin'. Boy along with her, drivin' a wagon. She was lookin' to pick up any calves we wanted to get rid of."

"She probably works all the herds that come up the trail this way," Matt said between bites.

"We let her have a couple that was just dropped. Have to get rid of 'em anyway. But if it'd been a man that asked for 'em, I mightn't've been so generous."

"Oh?" Matt said.

"That's the way it is, Marshal."

"Dolph, why beat around the bush? What's been your trouble?"

Dolph Quince curled his lip. "Jayhawkers!" he spat out, making a dirty word of it.

Matt swallowed a mouthful and chased it with a gulp of coffee. "They used to be a nuisance back on the Shawnee and the Chisholm," Matt said. "Haven't heard much about 'em this far west." The Western, or Dodge City, Trail was pretty well past so-called granger country, being mostly unfit for farming. It didn't give the Jayhawkers much excuse for operating, since they were, or claimed to be, farmers.

"Some of 'em must have decided to give it a whirl out here, whatever," Dolph said. "Whoever it is, they been givin' us an awful lot of grief."

Phil Jacks came over with a full plate. "Room for me here?" he asked.

"Sure, Phil," Dolph said; "find yourself a corner and squat. I been complainin' to the marshal here about the welcome Kansas's been givin' us."

"I've heard you can pay off them Jayhawkers to let you drive through," Phil Jacks observed. "Couple dollars a head, it takes."

"That'd only crease us for about six thousand dollars which we haven't got," Dolph growled. "Anyways, I wouldn't agree to pay 'em one nickel—a head or *in toto*, like they say."

"Well, they ain't asked us yet," Phil conceded. "First one that does, I'll shoot him, boss."

"Marshal," Dolph Quince said earnestly, "every last dollar I got's sunk in these cows. My relatives' and friends', too. We've come a long way, from the San Saba, and I'm aiming to reach Dodge and sell the most of 'em there. Then I'm supposed to take five hundred of 'em on to Major North in Ogallala. Him and Bill Cody're startin' a new spread up on the Dismal River and they're countin' on gettin' some good stockers from me."

"Sounds promising, Dolph."

"Well, you can see why I don't want to lose out on the deal now."

"Dolph, I don't quite see what I can do to help you."

"Couldn't you raise a posse?"

Matt threw up his hands. "For this kind of work? There'll be dozens of herds coming up the trail, from now to September. Talk sense, man."

Dolph Quince was silent for a minute. Then: "Well, will you ride with us a few days, get to know the boys some? We been harassed so much the last few days they're steamin' mad. I'm afraid that when we hit Dodge they're goin' to try for some Kansas scalps."

"I'm here now, and I've got to get back to Dodge," Matt said simply. "I'll ride along with you."

"Good." The trail boss yawned and stretched. "Man, am I beat! Soon's I get to Dodge I'm goin' to hire me a bed and sleep for forty-eight hours."

One of the men came up. "Dolph, there's a feller over here come ridin' in from the west a few minutes ago. Said he was lookin' fer a job. I told him to eat first, then he could ask you."

"He must be crazy," Dolph snorted. "Where is he, Joe?"

"Yonder," Joe said. "I'll fetch him."

"Dolph," Matt said, "I'd like to stand a guard tonight."

"No need for that," the trail boss answered, surprised.

"If you want me to ride with you you'll have to let me do my share of the work."

"All right then," Dolph said tolerantly. "Go out with the second watch if you want. Wrangler'll give you a hoss."

Joe approached them again. "Here he is, Dolph." Then addressing the man he had in tow: "This is Mr. Quince."

A thin, angular man with a long face stepped up. "Mr. Quince . . ."

"Quince is enough," the trail boss said gruffly.

"My name's Studer," the man said. "Carl Studer."

"Joe said you wanted a job; well, I can't help you there."

"Thought mebbe you could use a hand," Studer whined.

"Not much," Dolph said. "We've only got about four days' drive to Dodge."

"That much'd help."

"You must be mighty hungry."

"Well, I am. I'm jest about at the end o' my rope."

"Guess you can go along with us to Dodge," Dolph gave in. "Give the wrangler a hand. I can't pay you anything but you can have all the food you can hold."

"Thanks, Mr. Quince!"

"Come to think of it, we might need a hand to help drive some head on to Ogallala. I ain't sure how many of the boys'll want to go on past Dodge. Let's see how you do the next few days and then I'll let you know in Dodge."

"Gosh, all right, Mr. Quince; glad to."

"Where you from, Studer?"

"Colorado."

"Glad you ain't a Kansan; boys might have it in for you

if you was. Roll your soogan close by the wagon somewhere, and be ready to go out on third watch."

"All right," Studer said. "G'night." He walked off.

"Kind of a man that spends his whole life lookin' for salt
pork and sundown," Dolph Quince remarked, looking after
him.

"Let's hope that's all he's looking for," Matt rejoined.

"What you mean, Marshal?" Dolph swung his big head.

"Nothing special, Dolph; just a habit I have of not trusting
everybody on sight."

"You don't trust this fella? Seen him before?"

"He's purely a stranger to me, Dolph. But if you've been
having a lot of trouble, I just think it'd be smart to be cautious."

"Straight thinkin', Marshal. Anyhow, if there's anything
wrong with him, we've got him where we can watch him."

"Not if you put him on night guard, Dolph. If I was you
I'd keep him in camp except in daylight."

"All right, all right. I didn't figger you'd be runnin' the
outfit but I'll do what you say, Marshal." He laughed a little,
taking the string from it. "But you better stretch out somewheres and grab yourself some shut-eye. You'll be out singin'
to them cow brutes in a couple hours."

"Right you are," Matt rose. "See you later."

"Breakfast's at four," Dolph said. "Won't take you long to
stay all night at this ranch."

Matt had little chance that night to "get to know the boys
some," as Dolph Quince had put it. He rolled out of his
blanket in pitch dark to gulp a quick cup of strong black
coffee and ride out to the herd. There he and another guard
rode slowly around the bedded down animals, humming and
singing to keep them from getting restless, and doing his
best to keep all his senses alert and ready. Nothing untoward
happened, and a couple of hours later they were relieved
by the third watch. Matt satisfied himself that the new man,
Studer, had been allowed to sleep, then turned in again himself.

At breakfast the men all seemed to know that Matt had
stood one of the guard periods and they opened up accord-
ingly. A wiry redhead offered to return the favor by helping
him hold the lid down in Dodge when they got there.

"God help Kansas when ole Brick gits to policin' her,"

another rider quipped. "He'll have the gov'nor in jail and the gamblers runnin' the courthouse."

"Yeah but only the honest gamblers—meanin' the ones from Texas," Brick retorted quickly. "We'll give the rest up to ten to git an' then we'll start shootin'." He grinned at Matt. "I kin count to ten real fast."

"Ride into town with them boots off 'n' you kin be generous enough to count to twenty fer 'em," his critic came back.

Studer, the newcomer, looked glum. He complained that he hadn't been allowed to do his part by standing guard. Matt assured him that Dolph Quince thought he looked beat out the night before and had decided they could handle things all right without him. It didn't seem to convince him; probably he'd never heard of a considerate trail boss before, Matt thought.

After the cattle had been allowed to graze awhile, the men got them strung out and started on the trail. Riding swing with Phil Jacks, Matt began to forget he was a lawman. He hadn't done this sort of thing for years. Saddle work in the open air was the life for a man. Maybe he'd made a mistake going into law work. . . .

Dolph Quince rode up. "How d'you like bein' a trail hand, Marshal?"

"Fine as frog hair, Dolph."

"You like it so much, I'll trade jobs with you, Marshal," Phil Jacks said. "Know what I found him doin' in Dodge, boss?"

"Hangin' a rustler, I hope."

"Not a chance. He was settin' idle in a chair, soakin' in the sun."

"Well, I was in Dodge last year," Dolph commented; "I know he can move when he needs to. Marshal"—he turned to Matt—"you two crossed Crooked Crick on the way down. How was the sand?"

"Bottom's good where we crossed, Dolph."

"We'll cross there, then. Phil, you ride point and lead us to it. Take that Studer along with you."

"Don't need him along," Phil said.

"Well, I want him up front where we can see him," Dolph said. "He's with the hosses now; pick him up."

Phil Jacks waved his hand and rode away. The trail boss wanted to know about beef prices and conditions in Dodge

City. Matt told him all he could. Dolph looked relieved. The first big herd to hit Dodge would benefit from the present high prices being quoted. It looked as if his troubles were about over and he could forget the pinpricks of the Jayhawkers, if such they had been. Actually, Dolph seemed far from sure that it had been Jayhawkers stampeding his stuff and nibbling at the stragglers. A few renegade Indians from the Nations regularly got their hands on some trail beeves and sold them to railroad construction commissaries. Matt had never heard of any sizable gang of Jayhawkers operating this far west. He was inclined to think that Dolph had been magnifying his troubles. He'd been grasping at the easy explanation, no doubt, disregarding the probabilities.

Matt himself was more concerned with the new man, Studer. He got to thinking about Studer's reactions that morning. The more he thought about it the less he liked it. He spoke to the trail boss.

"The way Studer acted at breakfast," he said; "do you think it was natural?"

"Fella just wanted to do his part, I guess," Dolph responded. "Or anyway make us think he felt that way."

"It wasn't disappointment, though," Matt said; "it was more like he was uneasy about something."

Dolph looked at him without speaking.

"If he'd been sent in to look over the layout, maybe he was counting on clearing out during the night," Matt went on. "You spoiled it by asking him to stand watch. So he relied on us to wake him up, and we didn't."

"But he asked for a job, kept right on after I said no," Dolph objected.

"He had to have some reason for riding in on you," Matt said. "He must have figured you'd turn him down, but he wanted to hang around long enough to spot whatever he needed to know. By this morning he knew you had a lawman with you but he was stuck there and couldn't ride to warn his pals. No wonder he looked sour."

"Got 'er all worked out, eh?" Dolph said, but he looked serious. "Supposin' you're right on all this, what do we do now?"

"Keep our eye on him, like you told Phil," Matt said, gigging his horse. "I'll ride point, along with those two!"

"Send that cuss Studer back here," Dolph called after him. "I can use some help, and watch him too."

It didn't take Matt long to reach the van of the north-ward-plodding herd. Coming up to Phil Jacks and the new man, he gave Studer the trail boss's message. The man looked worried. He said he didn't think he could stand the dust back there. Matt told him he'd be on the windward side of the herd. He looked sullen but said nothing more. He reined his horse around and began riding toward the swing position, slowly. Matt watched him.

"What's the matter?" Phil Jacks asked.

"I don't know," Matt said, "but I think we may be riding into something. Keep a sharp watch ahead. I'm going to drift back toward the swing myself. I don't trust that fellow."

He let his horse laze along, then stop to nip at some bunch grass. Looking back as the longhorns moved past him, he saw Studer slowly approaching Dolph Quince. The trail boss raised a hand and called something to him that Matt could not catch.

Suddenly Studer pulled out a gun and leveled it. Matt saw the puff of smoke and saw Dolph's horse flinch, then heard the report of the gunshot. He urged his own horse ahead, pulling out his saddle carbine. Dolph's horse was going down and the trail boss was trying to get clear of him. Studer whipped a blanket from his saddle and, waving it, rode at the flank of the moving herd. Matt heard him yelling at the top of his voice.

The plodding longhorns threw up their heads, then broke wildly away from Studer. It appeared to Matt to be a fool maneuver but he could only assume that the man had con-federates near by who were in a position to drive a part of the herd quickly to a place where they could hold them.

He drove his horse toward Studer but the man was cleverly riding in behind the stampeding animals as they swung to the east. He flung a look at Quince. The trail boss was standing beside his downed animal with his sixshooter drawn. He was trying to get a bead on the dust-obscured, moving figure of Studer.

Men were galloping up from the drag. Matt heard shots from ahead, and leaving Studer to them, he swung his horse and hurried in that direction. He saw three mounted men tearing in from the northeast. They had emerged from a brush-bordered draw. Bearing down on the van of the herd, they were trying to turn the running animals more directly to the east. One of them was shooting at Phil Jacks, who coolly dismounted and returned the fire with his pistol steadied across the cantle of his saddle. The raider pitched off his horse and Phil turned his fire on the other two.

Matt got within carbine range and started banging away from his mounted position. The two jerked around and looked at him, then swung their mounts and headed for the cover of the draw. Matt pursued, continuing his fire. A horse went down and his rider hit the ground and lay still. The other made it up the slight rise fronting the draw and went over its edge, out of sight.

Matt jumped off his horse and ran up the incline on foot. Nearing the top, he dropped to all fours and crawled. He poked his head above the edge for a cautious look. Instead of dismounting to fort up, the man was running his horse for the east end of the draw. Matt took careful aim with his carbine and put a bullet in the horse. He wanted to take this man alive, if possible.

When the animal went down its rider hit the dirt, rolled over, and then scrambled frantically back to a position behind the still animal. It offered him poor cover from the marshal's higher location. Taking a chance, Matt stood up and started angling slowly down the slope in his direction.

He hadn't gone far when the call came: "Far enough, mister! Git on back now—you're in pistol range."

Matt judged it bluff, at the distance. He took a couple more steps.

"Stand there, I say!"

Matt took a few more steps, and stopped. "All right," he called, "put down and come forward!"

"Let me on a horse and I'll git outa here," came the reply. "We won't bother you no more!"

"I'm a U. S. Marshal," Matt called. "Give up—you'll get a fair trial."

"Nothing doing!"

Matt started walking again, carbine leveled. "Give up," he repeated; "you haven't a chance."

"I'm warnin' you!" the man shouted hoarsely.

Matt kept on. "I'm coming after you," he said grimly.

The man's head and shoulders popped up from behind the carcass. He snapped a shot from his gun. Matt's carbine spoke and he slumped back.

Matt approached with care. He got close. Nothing happened. The man was dead.

"You poor fool," Matt murmured.

Horses came over the edge of the draw, pounded down to him. Dolph Quince was on one of them; it looked to Matt like the animal Studer had been riding.

"You leave a bloody trail, man," Dolph said.

"Yeah," Matt said dourly. "Studer?" He looked questioningly at the trail boss.

"I downed him," Dolph said gruffly. "Looks like you walked right down on this fella."

"I tried to take him alive," Matt explained.

"There's nobody left to tell us what the deal was now," Dolph complained. "It don't add up to much."

"It was botched," Matt guessed. "They might've done better if they hadn't sent Studer into camp to reconnoiter."

"He might have made out, at that, if you hadn't been around," Dolph Quince rejoined. "See why I wanted you to come meet us now?" he asked, grinning.

Matt couldn't return the warmth. It was his job, and sometimes he had to take life to carry it out, but he never relished it. He looked up at the silent Phil Jacks.

"Phil," he said, "I smuggled a quart of wagonyard whisky out of Dodge when we started. The cook's got it hid in the chuck wagon. When the boys get those stampeded critters rounded up, you better get it and break it out. They'll need it."

"Thanks, Marshal. I know the boys'll take it easy when we hit Dodge, after what you done."

"All right," Matt said. "There's plenty of fun to be had, and you won't have to shoot anybody."

HOT SPELL

Sometimes Matt Dillon wondered if he was the right man to fill a marshal's job. Most of the other lawmen he knew took a simple view of their work. They were—or anyway, they represented—the Good. They carried on a kind of war against the Bad, which composed all lawbreakers, big and small. There didn't seem to be anything in between, for them.

To Matt Dillon, though, there was an in-between, and it was a sizeable one. In fact, when you thought about it, it probably comprised almost everyone. He had jailed a good many men whom he didn't consider very evil, or much of a threat to society. Some of them had got a wrong start and couldn't get untracked. Some preferred to take the easy way out rather than trying to make an honest living. Some actually liked the danger and excitement of a life lived outside the law. Most of these were not essentially vicious men—or they didn't act vicious, most of the time.

Once in a while you found one who seemed all evil. Not very often—no more often than you found a man who seemed all good. You *called* a man "good" if he was reasonably upright, kept his word with others, and practiced the accepted virtues most of the time. He could slip once in a while and nobody would blame him much for it, if he didn't slip too badly. If he did make a bad slip—well, Christian talk said *he* should be forgiven even then. The trouble there was that most professed Christians weren't really very *good* Christians—but that, Matt realized, was a part of the whole picture that kept worrying him.

Take the business of Cope Borden and Rance Bradley. In the simple division of things favored by most lawmen, Borden was one of the Bad. He wasn't one of the all-evil men— that extreme category that Matt Dillon seldom encountered— although he might have approached it. He was certainly cruel and arrogant and ruthless. There was probably little that he would not have done to satisfy his own desires and impulses. But in this *mix-up,* this Borden-Bradley business, what he did and what happened to him was not as troubling

84

to Matt Dillon as what Rance Bradley did, and what happened to Rance.

Rance Bradley was, by the *same* simple standard, one of the Good people. Matt himself had always reckoned Rance a "good" man. That is, he was reasonably upright, generally virtuous, and his slips had always been little ones. He was sober and hard-working and he had won people's respect in and around Dodge City. When he wasn't working he might come in to town for a drink or two with some cronies. He wasn't as generous as some people, but you could trust him not to cheat at poker.

One day, though, Rance Bradley fell from grace, not once but twice. He did it both times by trying to take the law into his own hands. Lynch law, to Matt Dillon, was no law at all —rather, the negation of law, so that, to Matt, Rance Bradley's offense was just as culpable as one committed by a common criminal. And, in both cases, his outburst was directed at Cope Borden.

Nobody in Dodge City paid much attention to Borden the morning he rode in. He was unimposing enough in appearance that he didn't draw a second look from most people. Those few who did look at him attentively saw a low forehead, a surly expression, and small, mean-looking eyes. He had a couple of drinks in a saloon, and when he went back to the street he found Rance Bradley looking closely at the horse he, Borden, had ridden in.

The horse was branded Bar Lazy B, which was Rance Bradley's iron. Rance couldn't identify the horse as a horse, but he had plenty of saddle stock and there wasn't anything distinctive about this bay mare that Borden had been riding. Anyway, there wasn't any question that it was burned with his brand, so Rance didn't lose any time labeling Cope Borden a horse thief.

In view of Borden's record as it was subsequently revealed, it all might have ended with a gun fight then and there, but Rance had several friends with him and Cope Borden was no fool. He laid a rough tongue on the rancher and asserted that he owned the mare. He either couldn't or wouldn't offer any proof of his ownership, though, so Rance and his friends started to administer some summary justice. Matt Dillon was supposed to be out of town so they must have thought they could get away with it.

They had Borden sitting in the saddle of the Bar Lazy B

horse, with his wrists tied together and a noose around his neck, beneath the projecting ridge beam of a livery barn, when Matt arrived on the scene and broke it up. He had returned to Dodge late the night previous, and no one but Chester and a couple of other people knew he was back.

"Rance!" he exclaimed when he rode up. "What do you think you're doing here?" He looked around at the others. "Jim . . . Ed . . . Frank . . . Tim . . . what's the matter with you?"

"He stole a horse of mine," Rance Bradley said, unabashed.

"So that means you can lynch him. . . ?"

"Hangin' a horse thief ain't lynching," Rance retorted.

"This heat must be getting to you," Matt said. "All of you. It's making you all act crazy."

Rance Bradley set his chin. "Somethin's got to be done," he announced. "We're here to do it. You got no right to interfere."

Matt stared at him, amazed. "Whatever's got to be done, the law will do it," he said. "If this man can't prove he owns the horse he'll be tried. He'll be punished if he's guilty. You all know me, boys. Now clear out of here. All of you. Go find some shade and sit in it. Cool off."

They all gazed at Matt, unspeaking. No one moved.

"You heard me," Matt said. "Get going. I mean it."

"What kind of lawman are you?" Rance exploded at him. "Interferin' with justice!"

"*'Justice'?*" Matt repeated. "You know better than that, Rance . . . Boys," he addressed all of them, "I'm not going to say it again. *Break this up.*"

They exchanged glances. Slowly they turned and drifted away—all but Rance Bradley. He stood still in seeming indecision. His eyes burned at Matt. Matt pointed at the sixgun tucked inside Bradley's waistband. The rancher's own gun rode in its holster.

"That his?" he asked, gesturing at Cope Borden.

"Yeah."

Matt held out a hand. Rance pulled the gun out and tossed it to the marshal.

"*You're* makin' the mistake," Rance said bitterly. "We could have handled this better." He nodded at Borden. "Look at him. You can tell a gunman by the looks, well's I can. Look at that holster. Look at the butt of his gun."

He jerked around and walked away, stiff-legged. Matt

watched him go, then glanced at the gun. There were several notches crudely carved on the butt. He shucked the cartridges out of it and tucked it into his hip pocket. Then he turned to Cope Borden, who had not said a word since he arrived on the scene. Now he spoke.

"I'm glad you happened along this mornin'. Ain't often the law gives me a lift."

Matt took out his knife and cut the rope from the man's wrists. Borden reached up and got the noose from around his neck. Then he dismounted.

"Say, what's your handle?" he asked.

"Dillon."

"Cope Borden."

"I've seen you before," Matt said; "seen your face on wanted posters, anyway."

"Any on me now, Dillon?"

"Not lately," Matt admitted.

"They shouldn't be," Borden said, his face hardening. "I just finished six years at Prison Hill."

Matt moved around so he could see the brand on the horse's flank. Borden watched him.

"I didn't steal this horse," he said.

"Rance Bradley brands with a Bar Lazy B."

A humorless grin touched Borden's lips. "Lot o' people use the same burn as that."

"Not around here."

"Who said I got this mare around here?"

"Well," Matt said patiently, "where did she come from?"

"Arizona. Bought her three weeks or so back, just before I left the Territory."

"Who from?"

"Horse trader in Yuma."

"He give you a bill of sale?"

"Might of." Borden's lips twisted. "I don't keep papers much."

"What's his name, then?"

"Ain't sure I can recall . . ."

"You'd do well to think hard about it," Matt said.

Borden thought. "Sampson, or something like that . . . no, Saunders—that's it, Saunders."

"Saunders," Matt said. "In Yuma."

"Yeah."

"Did you tell that to Rance Bradley and those others?"

Cope Borden sneered. "Them? Heck, folks like them I don't tell nothin'. 'Honest, law-abidin' citizens', I suppose they call themselves." He touched his belly. "They give me a sick feelin', here in the guts."

Matt looked at him and said nothing. It was plain that Borden cherished the very resentment that he felt against ordinary, honest people. Probably he fed on it, using it to counter some secret desire to be respectable folks himself, an impulse that he felt he had to be ashamed of, and therefore fought against.

"How about my gun?" he was saying.

"I'll keep it," Matt told him, "for the time being."

Borden bristled a little, then relaxed. "Well, what happens now?"

"A jail cell, for you," Matt said, "while I send a telegram to Yuma. It'll be cooler than here on the street, anyway."

"Yeah," Borden said. "Maybe that's why I'm gonna let you put me in your jail, Dillon—so's I can get out of the heat. But I've had all I want of jails. I better get a fair shake, or I'll bust your egg crate wide open and I don't care who gets hit with the pieces."

"You're making pretty tough talk, Borden," Matt said coldly.

"Why shouldn't I?" he demanded. "You think I owe you somethin' because you saved me from hangin'? Well, I don't! You never done it for me, I know that. You don't like me. All right, I don't like you." He paused. "I just thought I'd let you know where we stand, mister."

"We can leave it right there, then," Matt said. "I'm afraid I don't want it any different, Borden."

When the answering telegram came in from the sheriff's office in Yuma, Matt was waiting for it in the telegraph office. He took the message from the telegrapher and read it. It confirmed that Cope Borden had purchased from a horse trader named Saunders a bay mare branded with a Bar Lazy B brand. The trader had got the horse from Dave Burns, who ran stock east of Yuma under that brand.

Matt stuffed the telegram in his pocket, tossed the man a half dollar, and went out to the street. He headed for the jail. As he passed a saloon he noticed Rance Bradley's horse at the hitchrack. He went into the place.

Rance was standing at the bar with a half-empty bottle of

beer in front of him. He mopped the sweat from his face with a blue bandanna as he talked to the bartender. Matt stepped up beside him.

Rance turned his head. A faint frown settled over his face as he waited for Matt to speak.

"I aimed to ride out to your place later, Rance," Matt said. "Now I won't have to."

"What's on your mind?" Rance said brusquely.

"It's about that fellow whose neck you were aching to stretch."

"Look, the last I knew I had two head of saddle stock missin'," Rance began; "then this hombre waltzes into town ridin' one—"

He stopped as Matt took the message from his pocket and extended it toward the rancher.

"Read this," the marshal said. "Just got it from Yuma."

Rance took it slowly. He read it through. His lips pouted out. He looked up and handed it back to Matt.

"Guess I made a mistake," he said sourly.

"Yes, Rance," Matt said; "you made a mistake."

"A natural one," Rance persisted. "Why, his looks—you know how a gunman looks, same as I do. I'm tired havin' so many of his kind around Dodge City."

"Well, I don't like his looks or his kind any more than you do," Matt said. "But he hasn't done as much as look cross-eyed here, as far as I know."

"Not here, maybe—but he's done plenty before now, in other places. I know the breed. You do too!"

"Rance, it sounds almost like you're mad because he *didn't* steal your horse."

He sniffed. "Look, I said I made a mistake."

"If you had lynched him, I'd be holding you for murder right now," Matt pointed out. "You might not be so lucky again. Put some thought on it, Rance."

Rance Bradley's face was flushed and angry as he stared back at Matt. The marshal continued to regard him for a moment. Then he put the message back in his pocket and turned to go out.

"*You'll* be makin' a mistake," Rance flung at his back, "if you don't run him out before he does pull something raw around here!"

Matt watched Cope Borden as he sat behind his desk and

pushed the man's gun across it toward him. Borden grinned as he picked it up, patted it, then dropped it into his holster. Matt handed him the telegram.

"It's as good as a bill of sale," he said, "in case anybody asks you about that horse again."

Borden read it and tossed it down on the desk top. "I got a better answer than that, if any of them 'honest, law-abidin' citizens' do ask any more questions." He touched his holster.

"Forget that," Matt warned him. "I protected you when your rights were threatened. I'll arrest you just as quick if I have to."

Borden leaned an arm on the desk and thrust his face close to Matt's. "You goin' to arrest Bradley and them other honest citizens?"

"I am not."

"They was breakin' the law, wasn't they?"

"They had you pegged as a horse thief," Matt commented. "You wouldn't go out of your way to prove any different."

"Dillon, I wouldn't give that kind the satisfaction of ex-plainin' anything! No matter what I said to 'em they'd've hung me just the same. I know them, I tell you!"

"I know you, too, Borden," Matt told him quietly. "You're a man that's had a lot of trouble. You can still have a lot, if you want it."

Borden stood up straight. "I don't want nothing I can't handle."

"Borden," Matt asked, "where were you headed for when Bradley and the rest grabbed you?"

"I was headin' for Missouri—then," he said defiantly.

"Got a job waiting for you there? Any family?"

"I got nothing there," Borden told him flatly. "Nor any-where else." He let a disagreeable smile stretch his thin lips. "Reckon I'll stick around Dodge awhile, Dillon. Now that you know I'm clean as a hound's tooth. I'll walk the streets along with all your other law-abidin' citizens."

Matt decided to run a bluff. "You can walk from one end of town to the other in five minutes."

"What's that supposed to mean?" Borden demanded.

"It means you've got five minutes. Get out of town, Bor-den."

"Tell me why I have to," he said softly.

"I don't like you," Matt said. "Reason enough?"

Borden beamed as if he had received a compliment. "Well," he said good-naturedly, "there's no law says you got to like me." His voice grew sharper: "But then there's no law says I got to leave town, is there?"

Matt looked at him mutely.

"Is there?" he demanded.

"No, there isn't," Matt said. "I wish there was."

Borden grinned at him. He cuffed down the brim of his hat and started for the door. He turned his head and winked.

"Buy you a drink, Dillon?"

Matt glared at him. Borden shrugged and went out. Matt sat down at his desk again. He ran his fingers through his hair. He wished to heaven he had some real excuse to drive Cope Borden out of Dodge City.

Before the day was out, Cope Borden hit the Long Branch. He had a couple of drinks and then sat in on a poker game. Jase Hughes was running the game. He wasn't a houseman but he operated in the Long Branch more than anywhere else. Jase was a young man, for a professional gambler, in his twenties. He hadn't been in Dodge long but, although Matt didn't think there was much to the man, he had a courteous manner and an easy grace to his talk that had led a good many folks to feel well disposed toward him.

Cope Borden didn't know any of this. It wouldn't have interested him anyway. The only thing that interested him, after he had lost a pair of big pots, was the way Jase Hughes was dealing. He accused Jase of dealing off the bottom of the deck, proved it, and—when Jase started to whip out a pocket derringer—beat him to the draw and put a bullet through his heart.

Matt Dillon reached the Long Branch within minutes after the gunfire echoes had faded away. There wasn't much he could do, despite his desire to get something on Borden that he could at least use to force the man to leave town. There were plenty of witnesses who testified, reluctantly, that it looked as if Jase Hughes had been cheating, and that certainly he'd gone for his gun first.

Borden was smirking by the time they finished telling Matt what they had seen. "You see, Dillon?" he said. "It was self-defense, no question. You'd 'a' done the same thing, in my place."

Matt looked at him searchingly. "You provoked him to

draw. You called him a cheat to his face, in front of every-body."

Borden sneered. "That's what any man would 'a' done!"

There was some truth in that, Matt knew. On the frontier, men acted directly. There was scant room for the niceties, the balance of thought and consideration that might uphold a plea of "provocation" in legal proceedings back East. Matt was on thin ice even thinking of it, and he admitted it to himself.

"It was self-defense, wasn't it, Dillon?" Borden repeated, softly, intently. Maybe he wanted Matt to deny it; he might have been wishing that Matt would try to arrest him, and thus force gunplay.

Matt Dillon never knew. The sense of truth and fair play that was in him spoke for him: "It—was self-defense, Bor-den."

Cope Borden's lips showed the ghost of a smile. He looked casually at those gathered around. "Good-by, gentlemen," he said, sarcasm and defiance festooning each syllable, and went out.

Kitty came up to Matt. She had been there through it all. "He didn't give Jase much of a chance," she said.

"I'm afraid he didn't have much of a choice," the marshal said.

"You going to devote your life to backin' up that gun-sharp?"

Matt looked around. It was Rance Bradley. The rancher's face was dark with an uncontrolled passion.

"That's no kind of talk, Rance," Matt said.

"Who was right about him?" Rance challenged. "I told you he'd pull something raw if you let him hang around Dodge, didn't I?"

Matt's eyes went to the crumpled form of Jase Hughes. "Maybe he's the one that shouldn't have been allowed to hang around."

"You call *that* the right kind of talk?" Rance threw back at him. "Well, I call it mealy-mouthed blather! Jase Hughes wasn't no Sunday School teacher, but he didn't go around shootin' people up!"

"Well, he tried," Matt rejoined. He was stung by the rancher's accusatory talk. "Jase must have known that if he made free and easy with the pasteboards he'd get called on it."

"I don't say he was an angel," Rance conceded. "What sticks in my craw is that he lost his life because we got a lily-livered lawman that'd rather coddle a killer than stretch the precious law enough to keep a town clean of crawlin' scum that's dangerous every minute they stay!"

"I've had about enough of that, Rance," Matt warned him.

"All right, I just want you to know where I stand." Rance looked at the other men there. "I don't figure I'm alone in this, either. You had your chance to keep the peace here. You muffed it. Now you're aiming to take the easy way out again. There's some of us with guts enough to stand up to a gunman."

He waved his hand and started toward the door. Half a dozen others trailed after him. Matt's gaze as he looked after them was a mingling of pity and indignation.

"There they go," he said to Kitty. "Self-appointed guardians of the law. If Borden only jumped on his horse and fanned it out of town I wouldn't have to worry about them. But he wouldn't do that. He wouldn't want anybody to be able to say he left Dodge in a hurry." He turned to a man standing near the bar. "Would you go look up Doc?" he said. "He'll take care of things here."

The man nodded vigorously and started out. Matt headed for the door himself. Kitty looked after him and her lips moved in silent sympathy. This day was a tough one for Matt Dillon. Sometimes the people he served got under his skin.

When Matt reached the street he saw at a glance that the situation was as he had feared. Instead of shaking the dust of Dodge City quickly Cope Borden had been taking his time. He'd checked his gear, inspected his horse's hoofs, led the animal to a watering trough for a leisurely drink. He had still to hit leather when Rance Bradley came marching out of the Long Branch with his little contingent of self-righteous citizens.

Now he was standing and facing Rance with a disdainful expression frozen on his face. Rance was posing spraddle-legged at what he probably thought was proper gun-fight distance. The others were spread out to either side of him. As Matt emerged from the saloon he heard Rance say loudly, "Get goin', Borden!"

Cope Borden had time to reply simply, "Make me," and then Matt was between them.

"Rance," he said, "forget this. I'll handle it."

"Handle, handle!" The rancher's voice rasped at him. "You forfeited your right to handle it. You let him stay here and get away with shooting down that boy. Now we'll handle it my way!"

"Get out of the way, Dillon," Borden said in a tight voice. "I'll take care of him, and his pals too. Just get out of line."

Matt walked up to him. "Sure," he said, "I know you could kill him. And I know one of the others would get you."

"You aim to let 'em shoot me down?" Borden demanded bitterly.

"No one's going to be shot down," Matt said patiently. "I was hoping you'd have sense enough to clear out before this developed. Well, you didn't, and now it's up to me to save your worthless hide."

The gunman's eyes brimmed with hate, but he let some of the tension run out of his body. Matt turned back to Rance and the others.

"Defendin' a killer." Rance Bradley's tongue coated the words with the acid of contempt. "We don't aim to let you get away with it."

Matt did not answer him. The men beside Rance clustered closer, their animus now concentrated on the marshal. Matt's quick side glance located Chester standing to one side of the crowd of watchers. The deputy moved up quickly in response to Matt's nod.

"Take Borden back to the office," Matt told him. "He'll be safe there."

Chester took Borden by the arm. The gunman shook his hand off but at a word from the deputy started walking down the street beside him, in the direction of the jail. Someone in the crowd hooted. Borden looked back over his shoulder and grinned.

Rance Bradley's voice matched the hardness on his face. "Don't think this ends it," he said to Matt. "I want him." He corrected himself, looking at the men around him: "We want him, I mean. We're goin' to get him."

"I told you once today," Matt said to them; "now I say it again. Go somewhere and cool off. Go home. Leave this to the law."

Nobody moved. He saw they weren't going to. He'd be a fool to try to run a bluff on them now. Without another word, he turned his back to them and set off after Cope Borden and Chester.

Rance Bradley had his last word. "That what you call law? Protectin' a killer? Turnin' your back on *us?*"

Yes . . . that was law. Protecting a dangerous stranger in your midst. Turning a stony face toward your friends and neighbors. Doing it to protect *them*—against themselves. Doing it whether they appreciated it or not. Doing it while the stranger laughed at you, mocked you for doing it. Holding up your head in the face of scorn and abuse. But most of all, Matt thought suddenly, protecting the law—protecting it against the onslaught of those who stood to gain the most by upholding it. . . .

The gunman and the deputy were standing in the office when Matt entered. Borden looked unconcerned and indolent. Chester was tense and nervous. As soon as Matt came in he went over to look out the window.

"Give me your gun," Matt said to Borden.

He handed it over to Matt, grinning, getting a big kick out of all this.

Matt looked at him in anger. "That's a good man out there. I mean Rance Bradley. He's worth ten of you, Borden. I never had one bit of trouble with him before, nor did any other honest man. Now, for the second time in one day, he's talking lynch!"

"Look, Dillon," Borden said condescendingly. "I ain't a coward. I'd just as soon take care of this."

"Sure. And shoot four or five men while you're doing it. You'd enjoy that, wouldn't you, Borden?"

"You called it," Borden said. "I ain't going to claim the sight of a little blood makes me sick. Especially 'upright' citizens' blood."

Chester turned from the window. "Better take a look, Marshal," he said.

Matt went over. Down the street he could see a small compact group near the Long Branch. Rance Bradley was the center of it. He'd gotten a rifle from somewhere. He had more men backing him now. At least fifteen clustered around him. Matt could see that he was talking to them. He seemed to be making a speech. He raised a clenched fist to emphasize points a couple of times, and when he did Matt could hear the others' blended voices growling endorsement. Finally he pointed a finger dramatically toward the jail and stopped talking. They let loose a ragged cheer.

Chester looked wide-eyed at Matt. "They gonna come down here?"

"Looks like it, Chester."

"Great bunch of law-abidin' citizens you got here, Dillon," Borden said. "Every time I turn around there they are, wantin' to kill me."

"Maybe they're all drunk," Chester said.

"If they were I wouldn't be worried about it," Matt told him. "They're sober, so I'm afraid they mean business."

"Should I put him in a cell?"

"Wait a minute." Matt looked out at the scene on the street. The crowd had come part of the way to the jail. Now they halted. Rance Bradley stepped forward.

"We want that man!" he shouted through cupped hands. "Give him to us or we'll take him—which'll it be?"

Matt looked over at Borden. The gunman seemed untroubled.

"Well," he said, "you goin' to let 'em take me?"

"Go bar the back door," Matt said to Chester. The deputy started for the rear and Matt added, "Bring the shotguns here."

"Hey," Borden said, "you're talkin' my kind of law now."

Matt pressed his lips together. He kept looking out the window. Borden laughed, a jumble of grunts and wheezes. Matt gave him an angry glance.

"Dillon, I'm likin' this! You have to do your blasted duty, no matter if you hate my guts. You have to protect me and you could stop a slug doin' it. But I reckon you're a good shot, so you'll get some of them out there too!" He winked at Matt. "Friends of yours, Dillon?"

"Shut your mouth," Matt said.

Chester came back carrying two shotguns and a box of shells. "All barred up," he reported.

"They'll have to try the front," Matt said. "They wouldn't sneak in the back anyway, the way they're feeling."

"How *are* they feelin', Dillon?" Borden asked. A second later all three of them hit the floor as a bullet smashed a window pane and whipped across the room.

"Does that answer your question?" Matt said as they lay there.

Rance Bradley's voice floated in from the street. "That show you we mean business? . . . You hear me, Marshal?"

"They could shoot this place up pretty good if they feel

like it," Borden muttered. For the first time he sounded a little worried.

Still on the floor, Matt reached out a hand. Chester gave him one of the shotguns. He took some shells from Chester and loaded the gun. The deputy loaded the other one. Borden watched them.

"Shotgun can tear a man up pretty bad," he said musingly. "I have to hand it to you, Dillon; you know what you're doin'. Let 'em get close enough and you oughta be able to down two with every shot."

Matt and Chester looked at each other. Outside, Rance Bradley was shouting again.

"You hear me in there, blast it? . . . I'm givin' you five minutes to hand over that skunk! . . . If you don't we're bustin' in!"

The others outside shouted their approval. Matt took a deep breath and set his jaw. Chester swallowed audibly. Borden started talking.

"All my life people like that 'a' been gettin' me arrested, throwin' me in jail, kickin' me out of town. Fine honest, upright citizens. Oh sure." He looked at Matt. "I never been able to get back at 'em the way I wanted. This is the kinda day I've had comin', Dillon—a lawman doin' it for me."

Chester crawled across the floor and raised himself enough to peek out the window. "Looks like they're gettin' ready to rush us," he said.

Matt got to his feet and went to his side. He looked out. Rance Bradley was tucking his watch back into his pants pocket. The rancher was keeping his eyes on the jail building as he spoke over his shoulder to the others.

"Come on. Time's up. He ain't going to shoot us."

Rance started walking toward the jail. Matt poked the barrel of his shotgun out the window.

"Don't come any closer, Rance," he called. "I'm warning you!"

The rancher checked his movement. "I give you five minutes, and the time's up. I said we'd bust in, and we're comin'." He took another step forward.

Matt's eyes narrowed. He nestled his cheek on the gunstock and drew a bead. Borden had got to his feet and was standing behind him. The gunman could not contain himself.

"Man, if this is law I like it!" he crowed.

With a muffled oath, Matt turned on him. He punched Borden in the face, concentrating all the vexation and frustration of the day into the blow. Borden fell and his head bounced on the floor. He rolled over but did not try to get up.

"Chester," Matt said, "how can I shoot people who never did anything wrong till today?"

The deputy stared at him. "What you goin' to do?"

"Unlock the door," Matt said to him.

Chester hesitated an instant, then did as he was told. Matt handed his shotgun to the deputy. "Watch Borden," he said, and opened the door.

Rance Bradley was close now, and the others were right behind him. They all stopped when Matt came out.

"Well, come to your senses?" Rance demanded. "Goin' to give him to us?"

"Yes, I'm giving him to you!" Matt said. He didn't raise his voice much but it crackled with the emotion he felt. "He's all yours—he's right in there, unarmed. Go on in and take him!"

They all looked at him, and then at the door. Some of them looked at Rance, and some of them at each other. Not one of them moved. Not one said anything.

"Well, what are you waiting for?" Matt flung at them. "He hasn't got a gun, I told you. Go on in and get him. Take him out, and string him up!" His eyes were hot on them. "Then I'll track you down, every one of you, and see that you're tried for murder . . . After that I'll turn in my badge and see if I can forget it."

He waited. Nobody moved, or said a word.

"Well, go on in!" he yelled.

They were shifting nervously. No one was looking at him now. Finally Rance Bradley cleared his throat. He put a hand out in front of him. He seemed to be brushing at something unseen that was obscuring his vision.

"I—don't know what got into me, Matt," he said haltingly. "Made me kind of crazy." He looked down at the ground. "I'm sorry . . . I guess it was the heat."

"I guess it was, Rance," Matt said quietly.

"I'm goin' home," Rance said. He turned to the others. "All of us better go home."

He didn't look at Matt again. He walked away, his shoulders drooped. The rest of them broke up, a few mumbling words of regret aimed at Matt. He lifted a hand to them.

After that, Chester and Cope Borden came out. Borden's face was swollen where Matt's fist had rocked him.

"His horse is saddled," Matt said to Chester. "Go get it."

When the deputy had gone, Matt turned to the gunman. "Now, get out of Dodge," he said. "All the way out. Keep on going. Don't come back, ever. This isn't the law talking now. It's me."

"Yeah," Borden said. "Sure." He seemed chastened then, but when Chester brought his horse and he'd stepped into the saddle the hard bright cruelty showed through again.

"You ain't so smart, Dillon. If they'd rubbed me out I'd never be no problem to you. Now you'll be wonderin' when I'll be comin' back."

Matt stepped close to his horse and looked up at the twisted face. "I said get out . . . and I said don't come back, ever."

Cope Borden let his gaze lock with the marshal's for a moment. Then he jerked his eyes away and reined around. He went riding off at a trot.

Chester wiped the sweat from his face and shook his head. "A man like him . . . and you had to defend him," he said sadly.

Matt looked somber. "You know, I was just wishing he had done something here I could have jailed him for." He reached for his tobacco. "It must be the heat, all right." He sighed deeply. "Let's go put those shotguns back in the rack, Chester."

OVERLAND EXPRESS

A man named Joe Bodry rode into Dodge City. He was a stranger to the place; no one seemed to know where he'd come from. He stayed long enough to let his name be known and to kill a man in a gun fight. His saddled horse was handy and Bodry didn't waste any time hitting leather and making his getaway. By the time Matt Dillon was notified, got to the scene, and asked a few questions, the fugitive had better than half an hour's start.

Matt and Chester got on his trail—Bodry had taken out across the prairie to the northwest—and gave chase. When it became clear that they wouldn't be able to overtake him in a hurry they settled down for a drawn-out pursuit. Matt judged that since Bodry had ridden into Dodge that same day, his horse wasn't too fresh, although it had enough left for an initial fast run. His estimate proved out. Bodry made it across the Smoky Hill River some ninety miles out of Dodge. There his horse played out and fell. Bodry forted up behind the downed animal and waited.

Matt and Chester approached close enough for the marshal to call to Bodry to give up. Bodry responded by opening fire on them with a sixgun. Matt, who knew Bodry had no rifle, had thought they were beyond effective revolver-fire range. Bodry proved a better shot with a Colt's than he had any right to be. Four shots and one minute later Matt and Chester were both crouched behind their own downed horses, Matt's dying and the deputy's crippled.

Matt and Chester were both equipped with saddle carbines. They pulled them free and got ready to put them into action. Matt didn't feel much like temporizing but he sent one shot a few inches above the spot where he judged Bodry had his head ducked and shouted a last challenge. It brought results. Bodry cautiously fluttered a soiled white handkerchief and called that he was ready to quit.

Matt told him to throw out his weapons. One revolver arched up in the air from behind the fallen horse and plunked to the ground several yards to one side. A second one followed. Then Bodry stood up slowly, his hands raised in the air.

Chester looked at Matt anxiously. "You think it's a trick?"

"I don't know," Matt said. "You keep him covered." He called to Bodry to stay where he was. He laid his carbine down, got to his feet, drew his sixgun, and walked slowly toward the man. When he was ten feet from him he called to Chester to approach. When the deputy was close Matt told Bodry to turn his back. He had Chester look him over for a hide-out gun.

"You satisfied now?" Bodry said.

"Yeah." Matt told him to turn around. Bodry was young, scarcely more than a boy. His face was unlined and pleasant-looking, close to handsome. That made no difference; Matt Dillon had met baby-faced killers before this.

"I'm sort of curious," he said to Bodry; "why didn't you shoot it out?"

"I didn't want to kill anybody, Sheriff," Bodry said.

"Marshal," Matt corrected him. "You killed a man in Dodge."

"He went for his gun, Marshal," Bodry said. "I had to draw. It was him or me."

"A dozen men saw it happen. Some of them say you drew first."

"Sure," Bodry said bitterly. "He had friends there. They were sayin' it the minute after he hit the dust. It's a wonder they didn't start sayin' it with their guns. Maybe because mine was already in my fist. Anyway, that's why I lit out."

"It made you look guilty," Matt said. "You should have stayed and faced the law if you weren't."

"What kind of a shake would I have got in Dodge?" Bodry protested. "Nobody knows me there."

It irritated Matt. "No matter what you've heard," he said, "we have some law in Dodge besides gun law. I'm a peace officer, not just a lead slinger. 'Lawman,' they call me, and I try to live up to what it means. I don't aim to see innocent folks punished. Or guilty ones go free, either. So you're going back to stand trial," he ended simply.

Bodry looked at him curiously. "Say, who are you?" he said suddenly. "You named yourself 'Marshal'—is it Marshal Dillon?"

"Matt Dillon, yes."

"Yeah, I heard talk about you in Colorado," Bodry said.

"You're all right, accordin' to that. Maybe I made a mistake . . ."

"Say, how're we goin' to get back to Dodge, Marshal?" Chester broke in. "We ain't got a whole horse between the three of us."

"We crossed the Overland route four, five miles back," Matt said. "We'll have to walk there and wait for the eastbound stage to come along. We can ride in to Fort Downer, borrow some Army mounts, and turn them in at Fort Dodge when we reach home."

Chester groaned. "I sure wish your horse had give out closer to the road, Bodry."

"Will it be all right if I lug my saddle back with me?" Bodry asked. "It's about the only thing I got that's worth much."

"Sure," Matt said. "We're not going to leave ours."

Chester groaned again.

Five miles was a long, wearisome walk for men accustomed to horseback travel. Packing heavy saddles made it worse. The three men reached the stage road stumbling with fatigue. They threw themselves down to wait. Matt had some water left in his canteen. They drained it. Bodry, who seemed surprised and grateful when he got an equal share, lay back, closed his eyes and went to sleep. Matt made sure that he wasn't feigning; then he and Chester cat-napped by turns.

Time went by. Matt was sitting up, his senses alert. Chester murmured in his sleep, then slowly opened his eyes.

"Think that stage went by 'fore we made it here, Marshal?"

"Get off your back and look down the road," Matt said.

The deputy jumped to his feet and shaded his eyes. "Yonder she comes!" he said happily.

Matt roused Bodry, who yawned and stretched the stiffness from his limbs. He squinted at the far-off, approaching vehicle. "Suppose they won't stop for us?" he said.

"Driver'll spot our saddles," Matt said. "He'll know we're not road agents."

"Marshal," Bodry said in a quiet voice, "you don't owe me nothing, but . . . well, I never been arrested before. I wish the people on the stage didn't have to know. I'd be kind of ashamed."

"What do you expect me to do about it?" Matt asked.

"Just don't let 'em know you're takin' me in," Bodry pleaded. "It won't make no difference to you."

Matt looked at him searchingly. "All right," he said finally. "I'm not wearing a badge, anyway." Bodry relaxed in relief and Matt added, "It's possible the driver or a passenger might know me, I can't help that." Then he warned, "You make one wrong move and it's all off: I'll hogtie you and make you ride on the roof."

"Don't worry, Marshal," Bodry said.

The stage was nearing them. The driver had slowed up a bit. The three could see a shotgun messenger perched beside the ribbon handler. Both of them were giving the waiting men all their attention. Chester raised his arm. The stage came on, more slowly. The driver pulled to a stop. He and the guard looked down at them suspiciously.

"Take a look at the gent ridin' beside me," the driver said warningly. "That's a shotgun he's totin'."

"He won't need it," Matt answered. "All we want is a ride."

"Where's your hosses?" the driver demanded.

"Lost 'em," Matt said, feeling like a fool. He hoped he wasn't making a mistake, protecting young Bodry this way.

"Ye don't look like greenhorns t' me," came in response.

"We're not," Matt snapped. "It can happen to anyone."

"Truth in that," the guard said to the driver. "I think they're safe enough, Hank."

"All right, it's your treasure box," Hank said. Then to Matt: "How fer ye goin'?"

"Fort Downer," Matt told him.

" 'Bout sixty mile, that is. Cost you fifteen cents a mile—you'll be crowdin' us," Hank said, take-it-or-leave-it. "Payable now."

"That's nine dollars." Matt reached for his purse.

"Apiece," Hank said.

Matt counted out two eagles and seven silver dollars. "That's high but we're in no spot to argue." He handed it up to the driver.

"All right," Hank said. "Git in. I dunno how the other passengers are goin' to like this," he muttered.

Matt had been conscious of eyes staring out the coach windows at them. He walked to the door.

"Room for a couple more in here?" he asked, looking in.

There were four men inside. One of them, a white-haired old man with a beaked nose and brilliant blue eyes, said in a cracked voice, "Anybody fool 'nough to lose his horse oughta walk home!"

"There's room for two here, maybe." The speaker was a hard-faced man of forty. His black eyes flicked from Matt to Chester and Bodry. "Not three."

"I guess you're right." Matt turned. "Chester . . ."

"Aw look——" Chester began.

Matt stepped closer to him. "Well, I don't want Bodry on top," he said in a low voice. "You'll have to ride up there."

Chester mumbled but gave in. He tossed the three saddles up and the guard stowed them away. Then he climbed up himself, complaining as he did so that his fare should be less if he couldn't ride inside.

"Overland guarantees a ride, mister," Matt heard the driver fling at him; "comfort's the passenger's problem!"

Matt grinned as he motioned Bodry to enter and then climbed in after him. They squeezed into middle positions on opposite seats, facing each other, Bodry flanked by the hard-faced man and the oldster, Matt by a derby-hatted drummer and a timid-looking Mexican.

Hardface looked at Matt. "You seem to be the boss of this outfit, mister," the black eyes bored at the marshal.

"You might call me the boss," Matt said mildly.

" 'D I catch your name?"

"I don't see how you could have," Matt said. "It happens to be Dillon."

"Zimmer here," Hardface identified himself. His eyes slid past Bodry, flicked at the old man. "Gramp here calls himself Gant."

The old fellow snorted. "My *name is* Gant, and I don't give a short hoot in Hades what any of you call yourselves."

Zimmer grinned. "Kinda crusty, ain't he?" His eyes inventoried Matt, lingered for a moment on the holstered gun. "What business you in, Dillon?"

Gant snorted again. He glared at Zimmer. "Godamighty, where was you hidin' when they passed the manners out?"

Zimmer's black eyes glittered. "I wasn't talking to you, old man."

"No, but I have t' listen—what's your name? . . . what's your business? . . . next'll be where you from, I s'pose! Huh!"

Zimmer leaned forward. He showed his teeth. "Now look, old man," he grated, "any more out o' you, and I'll . . ."

"Don't try to spook me, I'm too old!" Gant interrupted.

He looked at Matt. "Eighty-five mister—'d you believe it?"

"Well, no, Mr. Gant, I wouldn't." Matt welcomed the diversion. "I would never have suspected that."

"Knew Meriwether Lewis, I did." the old man said. "Met him in St. Louis after he come back from his Pacific expedition. Him and Clark went, it was. There was a real man." He glanced contemptuously at Zimmer.

"Now look who's doing all the talking!" Zimmer jerked out venomously.

"No harm in passing the time, Zimmer," Matt said mildly.

"*You* trying to mend my manners now?" he demanded.

Matt stared at him. What was rankling in the man? "Take it easy, Zimmer," he said.

The black-eyed man lapsed into a moody silence. Old man Gant rattled on, recalling days and men long past. Matt listened, occasionally putting in a word or two. The miles slipped by. Soon after dusk they rolled into Monument Station, an overnight stop. It was a long, low sod-roofed hut of crude mud-colored bricks. One end was an eating-room; the other contained several bunks for stage passengers.

After an unsavory meal of fat pork and poorly cooked beans, Matt and Chester took Bodry outside for a smoke. They leaned on the corral fence and rolled cigarettes. Puffing, Matt glanced at Bodry. The young fellow had said little during the ride. Certainly he had given no sign of wanting to escape. Matt was satisfied he had resigned himself to returning to Dodge and facing the music. Nevertheless he did not intend to relax his watchfulness.

"You said you came from California, Bodry?" He was referring to information the man had given while they were trudging to catch the stage.

"Yeah." Bodry seemed to be thinking about something else but he went on. "I was born in Sacramento. My old man was a Forty-niner. Never struck it lucky, though. He was workin' day labor on a town job when he died."

Chester announced that he was going to sleep outside. The building was poorly ventilated, and smelly within. "Fella'd suffocate in there," he said.

"All right," Matt told him, "but don't get too cozy. You'll have to stand guard over our friend here half the night. I'll watch him the other half."

"I'm not goin' to run away," Bodry said.

"Maybe not. I recall you did once," Matt said drily.

"Look, Marshal," Bodry's voice went low and earnest. "You don't trust me—yet. Maybe you've got reason not to. But I'm going to tell you something that'll make you believe me. Believe that I'm not an outlaw, I mean."

"What's all this, now?"

"It's about Zimmer—or this fella that calls himself Zimmer . . ."

"What about him?" Matt came alert. He'd been thinking about the man some, turning the problem over in his mind. It could be that Zimmer was just one of these naturally testy, prying men, always seeming to look for trouble. Still, he'd thought he'd sensed something more, a tension, a nervousness born of nothing that he could discern on the surface in the stagecoach, not the simple product of a long, wearisome trip. . . .

"Zimmer ain't his real name," Bodry said. "Or anyway it wasn't the name printed under the picture of him I saw tacked on a tree back in California."

Matt dropped his cigarette stub, ground it under his heel. "Go on, Bodry," he said.

"The name on that was Chip Ryan. I think the reward was five hundred dollars."

"You sure it was his picture, though?"

"That I'm sure of, Marshal."

"What was he wanted for?"

"Road-agenting—holding up stages," Bodry replied. "I heard tell how he operates. Or does sometimes, anyhow. Rides in a coach as a passenger, and when his pardners halt the stage, in a canyon or somewhere, he pulls a gun and cows the other passengers and takes care of the men on top if they're puttin' up resistance. They have an extra horse along and he rides away with them."

"He couldn't pull that very often, once his face was known," Matt observed.

"Sure not," Bodry concurred. "Maybe that's why he's moved east—California's on to him."

Matt was silent. Bodry might be telling the truth. Or he might be fabricating the whole thing. Again, he might actually have seen such a wanted poster and simply be mistaken about the man. Zimmer had seemed tense and unnecessarily irritated by the old man in the coach, but that wasn't much to go on. He might just be ugly-natured, a chip-on-the-shoulder fellow; the frontier had its share of such. . . .

Chester broke in on his thoughts. "You goin' to arrest him, Marshal?"

"Let's use our heads about this," Matt said, a little sharply. "All we have is Bodry's unsupported charge—that this Zimmer is really Chip Ryan, wanted in California for stage robbery. I've never seen a picture of Ryan. You've never seen a picture of Ryan. We don't *know* if one exists. Bodry here *asserts* that one exists. Come to that, we can't be sure such a person as Chip Ryan exists . . ."

Bodry started to protest.

"Now simmer down," Matt told him. "As a matter of fact, I kind of feel you're telling the truth as you know it. I don't see any reason why you'd be making this up—if it's untrue it wouldn't get you anywhere: probably it'd do the opposite. Still, you might be mistaken about it. Maybe your sudden zeal for righteousness is carrying you away. Anyway, I can scarcely put Zimmer under arrest on such puny evidence as there is. All I can do is keep an eye on him, till we reach Fort Downer. There I can try to check on him."

"The stage'll probably be held up long before we get to Fort Downer, Marshal," Bodry objected.

"If it is, those holdups will have a fight on their hands, Bodry. If it does happen like that I'm thanking you for this. For your sake, I hope you're telling the truth. Now, Chester, I want you and Bodry to go into the station. If you can speak to that shotgun guard without letting Zimmer overhear you, ask him to come out here where I can talk to him. Then you and Bodry start some talk with Zimmer and keep him occupied till either me or the guard comes back inside. Buy him a drink if you have to—here's some money, Chester . . ."

After Bill Berryman, the express guard, had come out and Matt had identified himself, the two held a rapid, whispered conference. Berryman divulged that the express box held almost $50,000 on this trip. The likeliest place for a holdup this side of Fort Downer would be at a spot called Willow Bend, about ten miles east of Monument Station, where some scrubby trees would afford cover for lurking men and saddle animals. Matt told Berryman to instruct Hank to tool the stage through Willow Bend as fast as he could. Chester would be on the roof to give him a hand and Matt would be inside to trump Zimmer's ace and organize the other passengers for resistance.

"Dillon," Bill Berryman whispered tensely. "You sure they're gonna try to pull it this way?"

"No, I'm not sure of it," Matt returned, wondering how much of a straw man he'd been so busily setting up. "I don't even know if they're going to try to pull it at all." If he was honest he'd have to say he didn't even know if "they" existed. "But you've been riding gun long enough to know we've got to play it safe, be ready for anything."

"Yeah," Berryman said. "I know."

"And Bill," Matt cautioned, "when you go back in, don't let on anything about all this. Or who I am."

"Okay," Berryman said grimly; "I ain't figgering to spoil our fun, Dillon. Only theirs."

Matt watched him go back in. Berryman would be all right. He knew how to handle trouble when it came. He went on living, and making fair pay, because he did know. When trouble came beyond his capacity to handle his life might come to a sudden end, along with his career. Matt Dillon knew a quick poignant hope that tomorrow's span would not encompass such an end for Bill Berryman. If, due to young Joe Bodry's warning, it did not, Matt would see that the kid got the full benefit of his move.

The Overland stage for Fort Downer left Monument Station the next morning after sunup. The Willow Bend danger spot awaited them, some ten miles ahead. Once past that, they should be able to look ahead to a presumably safe journey the rest of the way. Farther east lay a small station, manned by a lone stock tender, which they should reach in the middle of the morning. Horses could be changed there, but it was not a scheduled passenger stop.

Matt managed to get himself established on the right outside of the forward-facing seat. There he would have his right arm relatively free in case some quick gun work was indicated. Old man Gant was in the middle and Zimmer (unless his name was Ryan) sat on the left side. Bodry again occupied the center position of the opposite seat, between the derby wearer, whose name was Folsom, and the silent Mexican.

Zimmer seemed nervous, clearing his throat and spitting out the coach window on his side when he wasn't growling impatiently about the jolting they were getting—in fact, he seemed to Matt too nervous for an experienced road agent.

He wondered if the man had spotted him for a lawman, making him jumpy. Old Gant was less loquacious than yesterday; he directed a couple of comments to Matt but ignored Zimmer entirely. Bodry rode backward, his body swaying with the motion of the coach, his eyelids lowered as though he napped. Matt noticed that his legs were held stiff and straight, and hoped Zimmer didn't.

They rolled along at a moderate pace until Matt judged they had covered almost ten miles. Suddenly Hank, up on the box, popped his whip and shouted at the leaders. The coach gave a quick jerk ahead so that those on the forward seat had a hard time keeping their places.

Matt's eyes were on Zimmer. The man showed a fleeting surprise at the unexpected acceleration but no undue concern. He spat out the window again and snarled to no one in particular that the fool driver didn't know his business. Old Gant put his hat straight on his head again and allowed the driver was one of the best he'd ever known—and, likewise addressing no one in particular, pointed out that he'd "rid with a passel of 'em." Zimmer shot him a hot glance and muttered something that Matt didn't catch. Whatever it was, it made the old man tighten his lips, but he would not retort.

They passed what Matt estimated must be the danger area. The driver eased off the pace. Glancing at Zimmer, Matt saw that his face was calm. The marshal drew a deeper breath and let himself relax. He looked at Bodry, whose eyes were open now. The young man's expression was troubled. Matt began to wonder whether Bodry had been lying or just mistaken.

They jounced along. Matt tried to make talk but no one would respond except Gant. Even the old man seemed to have a check rein on his tongue, today. Perhaps he was nursing his rancor against Zimmer. After a while, however, he started to crane at the passing scenery and identify landmarks. Finally he saw something that led him to announce that they weren't far from the little change station. Immediately afterward Matt heard a shout from Berryman, riding above.

Matt leaned out for a quick look ahead. The station was in sight, a tiny one-room adobe hut with a corral near by. The corral was empty and there was not a horse anywhere in sight. A thin stream of smoke was coming out of the window facing them. Matt pulled back into the coach.

"Something's wrong at the station," he clipped. He had his gun out. "Be ready for trouble."

Zimmer was sweating. He started to pull his gun. "Hold it," Matt said to him; "too crowded in here." Zimmer glared at him. "Just have it handy," Matt said. Zimmer was agitated but he nodded and made no further move toward his weapon.

The stage was slowing. Gant cursed. Bodry kept his eyes on Zimmer. The derby-hatted Folsom's face was white and he was trembling. The Mexican turned his head and looked quickly outside. *"Indios,"* he whispered, and crossed himself.

The driver pulled and whoa-ed the teams to a halt. Matt heard him set the brake as Bill Berryman said, "What the devil!" and dropped to the ground. Matt opened the door and stepped out, trying to keep an eye on Zimmer at the same time. Once on the ground he shot another glance at the station. There were a couple of arrows embedded in the half-open door.

Berryman was stalking around, keeping alert. "Indians been here!" he said needlessly to Matt.

"Stealing horses," Matt said. "Wonder how the stock-tender made out."

The others were emerging from the stage. Zimmer was in the lead. He held his gun in his hand now. Gant was close behind him.

"C'manches!" the old man shrilled. "Look at them ar-ruhs!" He hobbled quickly toward the hut.

Zimmer grabbed his arm. "Wait a minute," he said; "let me take a look in there."

"We'll all take a look, Zimmer," Matt said. Everything seemed to point to an Indian raid, but he still had a nagging suspicion that all was not what it seemed.

The driver, Hank, fell in behind them. "Where's that pore devil of a stocktender?" he said nervously. "They kill him?"

"I'm afraid he's a goner, Hank," Bill Berryman said.

"C'manches for sure!" Gant repeated. "I kin tell them arruhs anywhere!"

They pushed into the hut. The light inside was dim, and vision was further obscured by the smoke that rolled up from a pile of stuff in one corner.

"Tried to fire the place but it's just smolderin'," Berryman said. "Look . . ."

The others saw what he did. Three men lay on the floor,

one apart from the other two. They stepped forward quickly.

"Ain't this the stocktender?" Berryman asked. "He's breathin'!"

"Yep, that's old Aaron," Hank said. "But who are those other two?" He took a step toward them.

Zimmer was there before him. "You can forget these," he said; "they're dead."

"Scalped, too!" Gant almost seemed to be enjoying it. "C'manches, I tell you—just like they always was, the murderin' devils!"

Matt doubted that they had been Comanches. Kiowas, maybe. They hadn't done any big-scale marauding since the Palo Duro Canyon defeat but small bands still went hell-raising once in a while. It didn't make much difference, anyway . . .

"Let's get the stocktender out of this smoke," he said. "Help me carry him out, Bill."

Together they got the frail old man outside. He groaned weakly as they eased him to the ground. His eyelids fluttered open. Matt saw the wound in the man's belly now, and judged he'd be out of his misery in ten minutes.

"It's all right, partner," he said. "The stage is here."

The man's lips moved. "Indians . . ." he whispered. "Didn't hear 'em . . . too late . . ."

"Ask him who them other two was," Hank said plaintively. "What they were doin' here."

"Leave him alone!" Matt heard Zimmer say behind them. "The man's dying!"

The stocktender's eyes opened wide for a moment and he looked at Matt with a terrible urgency. "Drink . . ." he muttered.

"Get some water, Chester," Matt said. The deputy ran for the water bag on the stage.

"Scalped 'em and stole the horses!" Gant was saying. "They'll never change, reservations won't ever do no good, you can't civilize redskins!"

Chester came with the water bag. Matt took it and helped the old man take a couple of mouthfuls. Most of it ran down his chin but he opened his eyes wide again and looked at Matt.

"Can you hear me?" Matt said.

His lips moved.

"The two men in the station," Matt said; "who were they?"

The wide eyes stared at Matt. A faint frown came. "Don't

know . . . come in, pointed guns at me . . ." The voice faded. "Was goin' to hide till stage come . . . sounded like they had partner . . . on stage . . ."

"Watch Zimmer!" Matt whispered fiercely to Chester. He saw Bill Berryman straighten up quickly. He bent to the old man again, demanding, "The partner—what was his name, do you know?"

The stocktender tried to say something. It came out a bubble. His eyes clouded, went blank, his slight frame jerked, went lax. There was the sound of a scuffle behind Matt. Bill Berryman cursed.

Matt let go of the dead man's shoulders and came around. Zimmer had grabbed Gant and was using him as a shield, his left hand a vise on Gant's arm, his right pushing a gun into Gant's back, as they moved backward toward the halted stage. The old man's face had gone pale, his lips quivered as he saw the menacing postures of those facing him and Zimmer. He moved his lips in a voiceless appeal.

"First one makes a move, I kill Gant," Zimmer said hoarsely.

"You know this tags you, Ryan," Matt said.

"Easy!" Gant said shrilly. "This fool's nervous!"

"Driver," the outlaw commanded, "you move over, slow, to the lead team. Take the off one's bridle and lead the whole shebang down the road till I say stop. Gant and me are gonna take the stage alone."

Hank looked helplessly at Matt.

"Better do what he says," Matt told him. "He'll shoot the old man, I'm afraid."

Hank moved toward the horses. Ryan backed away farther, trying to keep both the driver and the others within his range of vision. He stumbled and swore. Hank, near the horses, stopped and looked at him. He loosed a flood of profanity at all of them. It was going to be too hard for him to manage. Matt grasped at his opportunity.

"Listen, Ryan: you've made your play and lost. Give up now, and you face an attempted robbery charge. Keep on, and it will probably be murder."

The bandit glared at him over Gant's shoulder. "Who in blazes are you, anyway?"

"Matt Dillon, U.S. Marshal . . . Ryan, I tell you to submit to arrest."

"You ain't arresting nobody," he said, "unless you want

Gant to die, see?" He saw Hank take another step toward the horses. "Wait, you!" he shouted. He was going to lose sight of someone or other, doing it this way. "Get back there with the rest of 'em," he told the driver. "I've changed my mind. All of you line up. Stand apart from each other . . . then lift your guns out, usin' thumb and one finger, and drop 'em."

Matt played for time. "The westbound stage comes through here sometime today," he said. "You can't hold Gant in front of you forever. What do you think you can do when it comes?"

"He's right," Hank chimed in. "Be here not long after one. I drive it myself half the time, I oughta know."

"Never mind that," Ryan told them. "Do what I said. And remember, anyone tries anything, I blow a hole in the old man here."

Chester looked at Matt. "Think he would?" he whispered.

Matt said, "I wonder he hasn't done it by accident already."

"Come on, come on!" Ryan said fiercely.

"Better do what he says, I guess," Matt conceded.

"You first," Ryan said, "I mean you, shotgun."

Slowly Berryman pulled the gun from his holster, gripping it in the delicate way he had been instructed to. He dropped it to the ground and looked blackly at Ryan.

"You next, lawman." It was Matt's turn. He followed suit. He could see no alternative. Ryan held the high cards and there was no point in risking Gant's life. If the bandit made his getaway, which seemed in no wise certain, he would almost certainly be caught again later.

Chester tossed his weapon on the little pile. Hank, the driver, did not carry a gun. The Mexican also was unarmed. Somewhat to Matt's surprise, Folsom unloaded a small-caliber gun from his pocket and added it to the others. It came Bodry's turn.

He stepped forward. "I got no gun—" he started.

"Hold it right there!" Ryan snapped. "All right, I seen you was wearin' empty holsters when you boarded the stage yesterday. What's the game?"

"The marshal here took 'em," Bodry said. "I'm his prisoner—or was."

Ryan held silence a moment before asking, "What's he takin' you in for?"

"*Was* takin' me in," Bodry corrected. "No more. I killed a man in Dodge. They'd hang me for it."

"What's this 'is-was' stuff?" Ryan growled at him. "I ain't taking you with me, friend."

"Be smart, Ryan," Bodry said. "I can help you, you can help me." His back was to Matt. He moved his left hand behind and made a circle with thumb and forefinger so Matt could see it. "I can hold a gun on these men while you unhitch the horses. We'll ride two of 'em, bareback, and scatter the rest. Head north, keep off the road. It's our only chance." He spread his fingers, wiggled them.

"Bodry," Matt said explosively, "you do this and I'll run you down if I have to chase you to Canada!"

He was watching Ryan as he said it. Bodry must have been, too, as he said, "Better than hangin', anyway, Marshal. How about it, Ryan?"

The bandit realized this might represent his one good chance. He grasped it. "All right," he said. "Pick up a gun. Get over here."

Bodry bent and retrieved one of the discarded guns. "Bodry, I'm warning you . . ." Matt said loudly.

Bodry said, "I figure I'll live longer *this* way, Marshal," and stepped toward Ryan and Gant, who was still held in front of the bandit. "Unhitch the horses, Ryan," he said; "I'll keep 'em covered here for us."

It nearly worked. Ryan hesitated. Then he said, "No, friend, I think I better keep *my* gun on 'em while you unhitch the horses."

Bodry looked at him a moment, then stepped around the outlaw and the old man. Ryan put his attention back on the others, his gaze leaving Bodry. He was annoyed when he saw the smile on Matt's face.

"What the blazes you grinnin' at, Marshal?"

"Your new partner has his gun pointed at you, Ryan."

The outlaw felt a gun muzzle poked into his own back. "Drop it, Ryan, or *you're* a dead man," came to him in Bodry's voice. "I mean it."

"I can still . . . put a bullet in Gant," Ryan said tightly.

"You want to die?" Matt said quickly. "Or face a murder charge? Or—just attempted robbery?"

"Drop it," Bodry said again, behind him.

Ryan's face went bleak. His chin quivered, his mouth sagged open. His right arm dropped to his side, the fingers opened to let the gun they held slip to the ground.

"You're all right, Gant," Matt said to the old man. "You're out of danger." He squatted and picked up a gun.

"It worked, Marshal!" Bodry said gleefully. "By golly, it did!"

Old man Gant turned around and spat at Ryan. "I figgered you was no good, Zimmer!" he said. "Now you're headed fer jail, and I say good riddance!"

"Bill," the driver said to the express guard, "we got to put that danged fire out in the station. Them two fellas 're still in there, too!"

Chester had his own gun back now. Matt got out some rawhide thongs and the deputy tied Ryan's wrists behind him. Then Matt turned to Bodry. "I'll take the gun back now."

Bodry stared at him. "You goin' to take me in anyhow?"

"I am."

"It . . . well, what's fair about it?" Bodry said indignantly.

"Look," Matt said. "I'm not a judge. I'm a marshal. You'll get a fair trial. I'll testify to what you've done here. It ought to go all right for you, Bodry. Now give me the gun."

"All right, Marshal." Bodry handed it over. "I—well, thanks."

"Thanks?" Matt said. "All I did was my job. I'm thanking you."

THERE NEVER WAS A HORSE . . .

Kin Creed came from Arizona, where he was widely but not favorably known. He made more or less of a living at the gaming tables, seeming to be a proficient if not professional gambler. He had probably engineered a few holdups in his time, too; it was suspected but never proved. What he took pride in and apparently drew sustenance from was his skill with a six gun. He was said to be both fast and accurate, a combination that wasn't often found. What made him most dangerous, of course, was that he liked to kill. The positive enjoyment that he derived from taking human life helped him scale the ladder leading to the top of the gunmen's world. No moral compunction, no sense of guilt, hampered his rise.

Matt Dillon had heard of Kin Creed, though he had never seen the man. When he learned that Creed was in Dodge City, it was with a sense of apprehension. Not for himself especially, although a lawman anywhere in the vicinity of a gunman like Creed was, in a sense, fair game. If Creed were only passing through, the town might see him leave with no casualties in his wake. If he chose to stay awhile, the chances of doing so were mighty slim.

Matt's estimate proved over-optimistic. Creed shot and killed a drunk in the Long Branch the very afternoon he arrived in Dodge. Creed had, characteristically, announced who he was while he was standing at the bar waiting for his first drink. He always liked the effect he could cause by revealing his identity. It was more explosive than usual this time, but he knew how to handle it. Insensitized to danger by the liquor he'd consumed, a cowboy at the bar directed a couple of loud-mouthed questions at Creed. The gunman told him contemptuously to go milk his cows. The drunk turned away as though to leave, Creed reached for his drink, and the cowboy lurched back around with his gun in his hand. He made the mistake of announcing that he was the man who was going to kill Kin Creed. Five seconds later he

116

was lying dead on the floor and Creed was standing over him with his own Colt's smoking. It was quite a demonstration.

Matt Dillon came running into the place almost before the echo of the gunshot died away. He had his own gun out.

"Put it away, mister," he said to Creed.

"Who're you, now?" the gunman asked, although he must certainly have known.

Matt told him, and Creed said, "Well, you ain't arresting me; this was self-defense."

Matt glanced at Sam O'Brien, behind the bar, and Sam had to tell the truth of it. "He's right, Marshal. Pony there had his gun drawed and said he was gonna pull trigger before this hombre went for his own iron." He shook his head.

"All right," Matt said, looking back at Creed.

The gunman put his gun back in leather. Matt did the same and after seeing that the victim's body was taken care of, turned back to the newcomer.

"I heard Kin Creed was in Dodge," he said. "I suppose you're him."

"Yeah, I'm Kin Creed. From Arizona."

"You get run out?" Matt's question was only half sarcasm. Creed was tough but he wasn't the only fast gun in Arizona.

Creed's eyes narrowed. "Well now, Marshal, nobody runs me out of anywheres," he said. "Includin' Dodge," he added.

"You make any more trouble here, and I'll run you out," Matt told him.

"I've heard you was handy with a gun," Creed said softly.

"I don't use it to show off with but sometimes it comes in handy on this job," Matt said. "Creed, I just don't like your kind. If you don't leave town soon I'll be looking for a chance to run you out."

"Marshal, it didn't mean nothing to me to shoot that drunk they just carried out," Creed said smugly. "I ain't going to count *him.*"

"I don't like that kind of talk," Matt warned him. "You have the right to protect yourself while you're here, *but that's all*. Don't forget that."

"You know," Creed said, "I think I'm gonna like it here in Dodge."

Matt and Chester discussed the problem in the marshal's office later. Chester, who had talked to some of the people who had witnessed the shooting, reported that the gunman had drawn and fired with blinding speed.

"You can believe that, Chester," Matt said. "This man Creed has a reputation for good reasons. I've heard other lawmen talk about him. Hickok says he never saw anyone faster."

"Phew," Chester said in awe.

"But a man has to be accurate, too, or the speed is wasted."

Chester thought about that. "Well . . . he killed that fellar."

"They were standing close to each other," Matt said. "He just drew and fired."

"You figure it was luck then? That he hit him?"

"I don't know," Matt said slowly. "They say Creed's a sure-hit . . . but I'd like to see him hit a target fifteen feet away on a quick draw."

Chester gazed at him and concern built on his face. "You sound—uh—say, are you *worried*, Marshal?"

"Creed has killed quite a few men, Chester. That's all he cares about, what he lives on. He's all twisted, filled with hate. He vents some of it every time he kills a man, I suppose, but he'll never rid himself of it that way. Besides, he likes the reputation it builds for him. He said he wouldn't count that fellow back there, meaning it wasn't a kill to make him proud . . ."

Chester waited.

"But he'd like to kill me, he meant. That would make him proud."

"You think he'll try, Marshal?"

"Yes," Matt said. "He'll try . . ."

"Well, why don't you march right out and shoot him down?" Chester demanded fiercely.

"I'm an officer of the law, Chester, I'm not a gunfighter." He said it as a reprimand. "Do you think I should risk my life to satisfy Kin Creed's bloodlust, or his crazy ambition? I don't believe the taxpayers are hiring me for that."

Chester was contrite. "I just wasn't thinkin', I guess."

"If he breaks the law I'll have to go after him," Matt said. "And 'going after' someone like Creed means gunplay for sure. But I'm not about to put my life on the line as a sop to his reputation—if Creed can beat me . . ."

"Well, no," Chester said. "Wish the cuss 'd pull his freight out of here, though."

"It's not very likely he will," Matt said with a sigh.

Chester was searching for a way out. "Maybe if you was to send a telegram to Hickok, he'd come along for a visit," he offered.

"Chester," Matt said gravely, "do you think I'm afraid of Kin Creed?"

"No, now," the deputy said quickly, defensively, "but maybe he'd just sort of leave town if he thought he had to face both of you . . ."

"That's all right, Chester. Maybe I am afraid of Kin Creed. But if I know his kind, he'd never leave then, even if he would otherwise. That wouldn't make any sense. Hickok's needed right where he is."

"That's right," Chester assented.

"Maybe he can beat me, Chester. I don't know. I don't like the idea of dying very much. But it's not something that just came to me since Kin Creed showed up. It's something I've learned to live with for quite a while now." He took a deep breath and stood up. "Why worry about it? Let's look up Doc. He said he'd have supper with us tonight."

The three of them were almost finished with their meal when the restaurant door banged open and Kin Creed came in. He stood still for a moment and looked around. His gaze fell on their table and his lips twisted into the semblance of a grin. He clumped toward them in his high-heeled boots, his sloping shoulders moving in a slight graceful swagger. He stopped a yard away, his eyes on Matt.

"Evening, Marshal," he said.

Matt's tone conveyed nothing. "Hello, Creed."

The gunman's eyes moved to Chester—"The deputy," he said—and slid on to Doc. "They tell me this is the Doc," he said. "How're yuh, Doc?"

"Dr. Adams to you," Doc said. "I am fit, sir." He forked pie into his mouth, chewed.

Creed cuffed back his hat and looked sly. "You practice on horses or people, Doc?"

Doc swallowed his mouthful. "Sometimes," he said, looking straight at Creed, "I prefer horses."

The gunman stiffened and the slyness was supplanted by a

hard-eyed stare. "I don't know that I like that!" he said harshly.

"Just leave him be, Creed, if you don't like truth-telling," Matt said. "What do you want, anyhow?"

Creed's gaze swung to the marshal, then back to Doc. "I don't like croakers," he said. "They kill people too slow."

Doc seemed unperturbed. "You may come whining to me for help some day," he said, and wiped his lips with a napkin.

"Too bad you don't pack a gun," Creed said viciously.

"Creed, that's enough!" Matt spoke sharply.

The gunman put all his interest on Matt. "Marshal's got a gun, though," he said, almost as if reminding himself.

"Get out of here," Matt said peremptorily.

Creed took a step back. He was well clear of the table, but still close. "You calling me?" he said, a hint of eagerness in his voice.

Matt said nothing. Creed waited tensely. "Go ahead," he prompted. "Go ahead . . . go on, draw . . ."

Matt felt the fine beading of moisture that formed on his forehead and around his eyes. His voice was low-pitched and steady. "No," he said. "Not this time, Creed."

The gunman looked at him a moment longer. He let his body relax, then. He grinned and set his hat back straight on his head.

"Some other time, then," he said. "Invitation stands, Marshal." He turned his head and spat through his teeth. "Any time you say." He walked to the door and went out.

Doc Adams looked at the marshal. "Sorry I got you into that, Matt."

Matt laughed shortly. "It wasn't you, Doc. He's just trying to bait me into a gun fight."

"But why?" Doc asked.

"Maybe so he can say he killed Matt Dillon," Matt said bitterly. "But there may be other reasons. Look, Doc, he's a notch-crazy fool . . . Let's get out of here, if you're through."

Outside, the three broke up. Chester went to the jail. Matt made his first rounds, then took a break. He went into the Long Branch and saw Kitty at a table. He went over and sat down. He answered her greeting, refused her suggestion of a drink. She looked at him.

"Matt," she said, "they're talking . . ."

"Who's talking about what?" he said shortly.

"A lot of people. About you and that Creed. The talk is he backed you down at the restaurant tonight."

"I can't stop the talk."

"I just thought you ought to know, Matt," she said.

"Well, sure," Matt said. "Thanks, Kitty."

"What did happen, Matt?"

He did not answer immediately. His face had an inward look. Finally he spoke, slowly. "Well, I guess you might say it was true. Yes . . . he backed me down."

It was her turn to be silent. Then: "You've got a reason for letting him, then."

"No," he said; "not a personal one, anyhow."

"Matt, sometimes I don't understand you—" her eyes were anxious—"not one little bit."

"Try to understand Kin Creed," Matt said. "His reasons." He rolled a cigarette carefully. "It's his play, all this is. Not mine." He looked at her. "He been in here tonight?"

"In and out. Prowling, sort of. Didn't buy a drink. Didn't stay long enough."

He lit his smoke, took a drag. "Hunting for me, probably."

She looked toward the door. "He's found you. Just came in again . . . heading over here now."

"All right," Matt said. He waited, then looked up as the gunman stopped by the table.

"Saw you over here, Marshal," Creed was looking at Kitty. "Introduce me?"

"You can drink at the bar, Creed," Matt told him. "Plenty room over there."

"Now that ain't friendly." His eyes stayed on the girl. "My name's Kin Creed."

She looked over her shoulder. "Did somebody ask?"

Creed chuckled. "Hey, I like 'em peppery," he said.

"Beat it," she said in a flat voice.

"Sure, kid." He grinned and winked at her. "Get rid o' your friend here, and you and me can get together later."

"That's enough, Creed." Matt looked up at him as he snubbed out his cigarette.

The gunman's attention went entirely to Matt. "Now, Marshal?" he said, letting his lips slide tight across his teeth.

"You want me to draw on you," Matt said it simply, his face expressionless.

"You're catchin' on, Marshal," Creed said. "Slow, but you're doin' it."

"I don't intend to, mister," Matt told him.

Creed's voice went hard. "And I intend you will, sooner or later. Somethin'll make you. I'll think of it."

"Do your thinking at the bar," Matt said.

"I'll do that, Marshal." He turned to Kitty. "See you later," he said, and walked to the bar.

"I don't understand this, Matt," Kitty said after Creed had gone.

"It's simple enough, though."

"You're—not afraid of him," she said doubtfully.

"If I was afraid of his breed, I'd have to get out of the law business."

"He seems awfully sure of himself," she said, her voice showing concern.

"With some reason," Matt said. "He's a fast draw. One of the fastest. He thinks he can kill me. He's willing to gamble on it, to fatten his reputation . . . and to feed the hungry devil that's in him. I can't afford to respond to that. I'm not interested in trying—no matter what people say . . . Do you understand that, Kitty?"

She put her hand on his. "I'm trying to, Matt," she said. "But you're in a bad spot."

"Yes, I am." He stood up. "And the pay is poor, too."

"I'll speak to the city fathers about it," she said, forcing the brightness.

"Thank you kindly, ma'am," he said, smiling a little for the first time.

"Any time, Marshal." She gave him a mock salute.

He knew that it wouldn't take Creed long to force the issue. Plenty of opportunities for breaking the law existed in Dodge City. It happened the next day, in the Alafraganza. Summoned there, Matt found a man stretched out on the floor. He hadn't been shot. His scalp had been laid open by a heavy blow. He was unconscious and breathing heavily.

Matt looked at the anxious-faced barman. "Who did this?"

"Kin Creed."

"Where is he?"

"Went out the back 'fore you got here."

"What started the fight?"

"Well, there wasn't no real fight. This fella was standin'

here, drinkin' peaceful, wasn't payin' no attention to Creed. All at once, Creed pulls his gun, yanks the guy around, and bends the barrel over his head."

"I see," Matt said.

"No blame sense to it, Marshal. Just meanness, I guess. That Creed's ornery as they come, you ask me."

"You'd better send for the Doc. This man may be hurt pretty bad."

"Okay . . . Jimmy, run fer Doc Adams!"

Matt looked out the back door of the place. No one was in sight. He went down the alley to the street. There was no sign of Creed. The man could be in any one of a dozen places, waiting for Matt to come for him. Matt decided to let him wait longer. Maybe the tension would affect the gunman. Might as well pile it on. He walked to the jail. Chester was in the office.

"Well, Creed's got his fight," Matt said.

"You mean with you?" The deputy came alert.

"He pistol-whipped a fellow. No provocation. Guess why he did it."

"You think he'll submit to arrest?" Chester asked.

"Do you, Chester?"

"No, I guess he wouldn't."

"I guess he wouldn't, too. But it's up to me to stop him now."

"We could get out the shotguns," Chester said tentatively.

"You know I don't like to use a shotgun in town, Chester. Too much risk of someone else getting hit besides the target —and if you get close enough to eliminate that you might as well be packing a hand gun."

"I don't like you having to shoot it out with a man like him, Marshal," Chester complained.

"Well, I've got to stop it now," Matt said. "If this didn't work it for him, he'd kill somebody next. I can't very well stand by and see an innocent man die."

"Well, you're innocent enough," Chester said; "you haven't done anything!"

"There is a slight difference, you know," Matt said reprovingly. "You might say I'm neither innocent nor guilty. Sort of neutral—being the law. Anyway, Chester, he hasn't killed me yet."

"Now no—I didn't mean he has!" the deputy said loudly.

"And he won't, either." He looked miserable. "You—uh—don't figure he could, do you?"

"Remember, Chester," Matt said; "there was never a horse that couldn't be rode . . ."

". . . nor a man that couldn't be throwed!" Chester finished. It seemed to bring the deputy comfort. He opened the door and looked up and down the street.

Matt was checking his gun. He put it back in the holster, eased it out, dropped it in lightly.

"He's fast," he said musingly. "Fast. Maybe that's not enough . . . and maybe it is . . ."

"He's out there now," Chester said. "In the street."

"Is he standing still?" Matt asked.

"He's startin' to walk this way. He must've seen you come here."

"All right," Matt said. He went to the door. "You keep out of it, Chester," he said.

"Yeah, if you say so," Chester said.

"I do say so," Matt said sharply.

"I said okay!" Chester's voice was high-pitched.

Matt said tightly, "If he downs me you can use your shotgun on him. Just be careful, if you do."

The marshal stepped into the street. Creed was pacing toward him, keeping to the middle of the road. *I was right,* Matt thought, *he couldn't stand the waiting; it made him nervous. I ought to have the advantage.* Creed was reputed to be accurate as well as fast but his aim might be faulty if he'd been feeling the strain . . .

"You lookin' for somebody, Marshal?" Creed called as he strode toward Matt.

"I'm looking to arrest you," Matt said. He was standing still.

"I'm comin'," the gunman said.

He was getting closer than Matt wanted him to. He yelled to him to halt. Creed kept on coming. Matt got off a last warning cry and drew. As he did, Creed went for his own gun.

They were still far enough apart that Matt thought a half second's careful aim would give him the advantage. He extended his arm to sight-aim-shoot. Creed got off a quick shot. The slug struck Matt's gun and sent it twisting from his hand. At the same time a piece of ricocheting lead grazed his neck.

He stood there, his right hand numb from shock. His left hand went to his neck and he felt blood. He looked at Creed. The gunman was watching him, his smoking Colt's still half-raised. He stepped toward Matt.

"I could kill you easy now, Marshal," he jeered.

"You won't, though," Matt said. "You couldn't do much bragging about downing an unarmed man."

"That's right," Creed said; "I couldn't. So I guess you better get you another gun, Marshal." He squinted at Matt. "What's the matter your neck? Piece o' lead nick you?"

Matt nodded. "I'll go have Doc Adams patch me up. Then I'll get another gun. I'll be back, Creed."

Creed holstered his Colt's and spat. "Take your time," he said. "I don't mind waitin'." He grinned at the people approaching slowly. "Have to show respect for the law, I always say."

"Your aim was off," Matt said. "You hit my gun by luck or you'd be lying dead in the street now."

"You think so, Marshal?"

"This scratch on my neck can wait," Matt said. "Why press your luck, Creed? Throw down your gun. Let me lock you in a jail cell. The charge will be assault."

"You're wastin' your time," Creed said. "Mine too. I'll be back after you in half an hour." He turned and stalked away.

Matt watched him go. He hadn't thought it would work, but the gunman's ironic joke about respect for the law had made him give it a try.

Chester came up. "You hurt bad?"

"No," Matt said. "Anyway, I don't think so. I'll have Doc look at it."

"If he'd shot you when you was standing there without your gun, I'd have finished him sure," Chester vowed. He was carrying a shotgun.

"I couldn't have stopped you," Matt said. "But anyway he didn't. Chester, there's a gun in my right-hand desk drawer. See that it's loaded and bring it over to me at Doc's, will you?"

"I could take this over now, Marshal," Chester said. "Your gun hand will be sore and stiff. Nobody'll blame you."

"Thanks, Chester, but I'll handle this," Matt said. "Bring the gun, like I told you."

The deputy turned back toward the jail, his face working. Matt headed for Doc's place.

"I saw it all," Doc Adams said as he had Matt sit down. He took a quick look at the marshal's neck. "I was about to come down with my bag."

"Good of you, Doc," Matt said. "It's not bad, though."

"Just missed the vein," Doc told him, using a swab. "You were lucky, Matt. *Real* lucky."

"Yeah," Matt said. "So was Creed. Makes us even."

Doc worked swiftly. He got the bleeding stopped and put on some antiseptic. "Sliced the muscle there a mite," he said. "Couple of stitches'll fix it up good as new."

"Not now," Matt said. "Just put a bandage on it for now. And hurry it up, will you?"

"What's this?" Doc said. "What's the rush about?"

"Creed didn't shoot me when he could have . . . but he's coming for me in half an hour, he says. I don't want to wait that long if I can help it. The neck might stiffen up."

Doc looked at him in disbelief. "What're you talking about?"

"It's the way it has to be, Doc."

"Then you're as big a fool as Creed is!" Doc snapped. "What about your hand, by the way? It'll probably be as stiff as your fool neck. Or your pride, either!"

Matt was flexing the fingers of his right hand. "It don't seem bad—yet. And forget the rest of that stuff," he added sharply. "This is my job, Doc. You can help by tending to yours."

"Sure," Doc said bitterly; "you go ahead and tell me what *my* job is. I'm expected to do that the way you outline it, I suppose—and then stand by and watch while that lunatic fills you full of lead."

"You put on that bandage and listen to me!" Matt said. He went on as Doc did as he was told. "He's fast, give him that. But he's too much on the speed. Unless he's right on top of me he'll be lucky to hit me. I won't let him get even that close again."

"He hit your gun, Matt," Doc said slowly.

"Luck," Matt said. "Pure luck. It isn't going to happen again."

Doc pursed his lips. "Maybe you're right, Matt . . ."

"It takes nerve to stand there and hold your fire for the

little second you need to aim, Doc. Creed has guts, all right
. . . but he hasn't got that kind of nerve, I swear."

"Well, I hope not, Matt." Doc finished with the bandage.
"Now let me take a look at that hand."

"It's all right, Doc."

"Let me look at it, blast it! If I let you tend to your fool
job, please have the decency to let me tend to mine!"

He bent over the hand. "It'll be stiffening, all right. What
it ought to have is an ice pack. No time for that, though . . .
what I'll do is bathe it with witch hazel. Soak it good. It'll
evaporate quick, your hand'll be dry enough by the time you
need to use it . . ."

Chester came in. "How is he, Doc?"

"Pretty good," Doc grunted. "Except for his brains. They
need to be examined."

Matt grinned as he took the gun Chester held out. He
spun the cylinder, dropped the gun in his holster. He stood
up.

"See you later, Doc."

"Come by afterward," Doc said. "I'll want to sew up that
cut."

"I'll be back," Matt promised.

"Sure." Doc patted his shoulder. "I know you will, hero."

Matt went out with Chester. He looked along the street.
"Don't see him," he said to the deputy.

"Maybe he's getting himself a drink."

"Maybe, but I doubt it. He's not that kind of fool."

"People are sure stayin' off the street now," Chester observed.

"It's just as well. You take cover too, when Creed shows."

"All right," Chester said sullenly.

"I ought to look for him," Matt said. "My neck's getting
stiff."

"Why don't you?" Chester asked.

"Blamed if I know where to start," Matt complained. He
pulled out his watch, troubled by the pain in his fingers as he
did so. "Time's almost up anyway, I guess. He ought to be
showing."

"Yeah," Chester said.

There came the sound of a shot. Matt swung his head.
"Where'd that come from?"

"Sounded like the Texas Trail," Chester ventured.

"Better go over there," Matt said. "I'll stick here. It might be a trick to toll me over there while Creed sneaks in behind me."

Chester trotted across the street to the saloon. He went in while Matt waited, scanning the street in both directions. In a minute Chester reappeared. He waved at Matt.

"Come over heah!" His shout sounded relieved. Matt crossed as the deputy went back inside. He could hear Chester telling someone to stand aside.

The marshal went in. There was a crowd of men in the place but a path was cleared before him to the bar. There in front of it lay a man's body. He walked toward it slowly.

"It's Kin Creed, Marshal," Chester said.

Matt looked at Creed. He could think of nothing to say.

"He's dead," Chester said.

Matt found his tongue. "Who shot him?"

Chester didn't seem to know. Matt looked at the bar man, who licked his lips and slid his eyes to the left. Matt followed his gaze. A short, red-faced cowboy took a step toward Matt. He held a gun, its muzzle pointing downward. He seemed half in a daze.

"What dya know," he said, his speech thick from liquor, "I did it." He looked around challengingly. "I shot Kin Creed." He turned back to Matt, his eyes slowly coming to a focus on the marshal. "Who you think shot him? *Me*. I done it."

"Give me your gun, cowboy," Matt ordered.

"Oh no," the man said. "Don't try to bull me. I'm a gun-man. Nobody takes my gun."

"Don't be a fool," Matt said. "Drop the gun and put up your hands."

The man's face worked. "You want it too, Marshal?" He started to raise his gun arm.

"All right, Chester," Matt said suddenly. The cowboy looked around quickly. He lost his balance and lurched. Matt had his own gun out. He laid it aside the drunk's head, not too hard. He slumped, his gun clattering down. Chester bent, got the little man in a fireman's-carry grip, straightened up, and started for the jail with his burden.

Matt got the story in a few minutes. The short cowboy's name was Chuck Carter. He'd come up the trail with a Texas herd, had been in town two or three days drinking up his pay. Nobody knew why he'd taken it on himself to gun

Creed down. As far as was known, he hadn't been a friend of the man Creed had pistol-whipped earlier.

"It wasn't a fight, Chester," Matt told his deputy after he'd left the scene of the killing to come to the jail. "It was like Creed clubbing that other fellow. Only Carter didn't club Creed, he shot him."

"Golly," Chester said, "I don't see how he did it, as full of booze as he was."

"Carter shot him in the back," Matt said. "Creed didn't see it coming, never knew what hit him."

"Oh," Chester said. "Heck of a way for a man to die . . ."

"Yes it is." Matt said musingly. "A heck of a way—but maybe in this case it was the best way."

Chester looked at him and Matt went on. "If Creed and I had shot it out, whoever came out of it alive would have been even more of a prize for some trigger-happy bum like Carter to murder."

"That'd have been you, I reckon."

Matt Dillon flexed his stiffening fingers. "I'll never know now, Chester. Maybe I ought to be just as glad I didn't find out." He waved his hand. "Watch the store," he said. "I've got to keep a date with Doc."

THE PESTHOLE

A conference was taking place in Matt Dillon's office. Doc Adams was talking earnestly, directing his comments to the three grave-faced men who stood before him. A nervous Chester fidgeted in the background. Matt sat straight in his desk chair, his solemn gaze on Doc Adams.

Tall Kyle Mather, exuding a faintly supercilious arrogance in his professional-gambler get-up, sounded antagonistic. "You *was* calling this food-poisonin', Doc. What made you change your mind so sudden?" he demanded.

Doc looked at him irritably. He seemed about to make an angry retort, but he did not. "The symptoms, Mather, the symptoms—" he began.

He stopped as Kitty Russell, eyes wide and face pale, entered from the door leading to the jail cells. She wore her gaudy Long Branch costume, partly obscured by the white apron she had tied over it. Ignoring the others in the room, she crossed to Matt and whispered in his ear.

Matt nodded, letting his face show nothing, and Kitty turned and went back. Doc and the others looked at Matt questioningly. He gestured for them to continue.

"What's this about 'symptoms,' Doctor? What symptoms might you be talking about?"

The speaker was Abe Botkin, a short, stocky man who ran a clothing store on Main Street. As senior member of the city council, he was standing in for the mayor at this meeting.

"I'm talking about high fever," Doc replied. "Nausea. Languid pulse." He paused, then added slowly, "Everything that goes with typhoid."

"Typhoid!" Mike Hanna, the silver-haired, heavy-faced proprietor of the Dodge House, sounded badly shocked. "You sure of that?"

"I will be sure, as soon as one of them dies on me," Doc said sardonically.

Matt pushed back his chair and got to his feet. Kyle Mather started waving his hands. "You should've waited for it to happen before you turned the jail here into a danged hospi-

130

tal and sneaked them Long Branch women in here!" he
snapped.

"Hold up a minute now," Matt intervened. "It's happened
already." They all stared at him. "Otto Richter's dead," he
said. "Kitty just told me."

They were shocked silent for a moment. Doc Adams
rubbed the back of his neck wearily. Mike Hanna cleared his
throat.

"As owner of the Dodge House," he said, "I want to offer
every co-operation I can." He looked doubtful. "Within
reason, that is," he added.

Abe Botkin rubbed his hands together nervously. "What is
the next move, Doctor?" he appealed to Adams.

"Discover the source of infection," Doc said quickly. "Find
the common cause that's leading to all these cases."

"Very good." Mike Hanna sounded suddenly hopeful.
"That'll give you something to shoot at . . ."

"Now don't get ahead of me," Doc warned. "First, we'll
have to go on isolating everyone who comes down with it,
just as I've been doing here. If that doesn't work, we'll have
to quarantine the whole town."

"Now wait!" Hanna blurted.

"Even if it means asking the Governor to call out troops,"
Doc went on inexorably.

"Hold up one minute now, as our friend the marshal says,"
Botkin pleaded. "You can't do this to Dodge City, Doctor."

"The trail herds are due to start rolling in next month,"
Hanna said. "Think what they mean to us!"

"Gentlemen, Dodge City needs that business," Botkin
added. He pointed a finger at Doc. "Without it, maybe we
all go broke!"

"Now look," Matt said impatiently, "Doc just found out
about this typhoid thing, he didn't invent it."

"Marshal," Kyle Mather said, "I got every dollar I own in-
vested in my place. I need trail hands with pay in their jeans
if I'm goin' to stay solvent. Treating sick people is the Doc's
business. Closin' people out of Dodge City is somethin' else
again!"

Botkin was suddenly conciliatory. "Now, now, gentlemen, let's not get excited." He turned to Adams. "You got
an idea, maybe, how it all started—this common-cause thing
you mentioned?"

Doc looked unhappy. "Flies . . . bad food . . . contami-

nated water . . . rotten sanitation," he said. "Who knows?"
"You're a doctor," Hanna barked at him; "you must have
some kind of an answer!"

"So far, I've got just one thing to work on," Doc said
slowly. "Ten days back, the five men that we have here ate
dinner together in Bedino's cafe. They were making plans
for the Germania Society picnic."

"Well, now we're getting someplace," Hanna said impor-
tantly.

"I always said Bedino was poisonin' half the town with
that filthy rot he calls chili!" Mather crowed.

"Not so fast," Matt said. "Lots of people eat there every
day. Nothing's happened to the rest of 'em."

Mather ignored him. "Close up Bedino's, then. Run him out
of town. I'll pay him a little visit tonight and tell him to shut
down for awhile. No more typhoid." He had it all solved.

"Nobody's going to do anything like that without a court
order," Matt told him. "Or unless Doc says so."

They turned to Adams expectantly.

"I suppose we ought to close the place up for a few days,"
he said, "so I can look it over, see if anything's wrong."

"I'll see that a court order's issued," Botkin said eagerly.
"I'll get it all ready for you, Marshal."

Matt nodded. Looking relieved, the three men started to
go out. Botkin turned at the door.

"Remember, gentlemen, we'd better keep this quiet. The
welfare of Dodge City may depend on it."

"What about Kitty and Big Elsie?" Chester demanded
when they had gone. "Couldn't they catch it from them
men, Doc?"

"We don't know much about typhoid, Chester," Doc answered. "The most recent medical textbook gives it eight
skimpy paragraphs. But it is known that there has to be a
common source of infection. That's what we've got to find."
He turned to Matt. "I'll go in and look at Richter. Then I'll
see about getting him buried."

"It's lucky he hasn't any kin to start asking questions,"
Matt commented.

"You said a true thing there," Doc responded gravely.
"Nothing can start a panic any faster than the little word
'plague.' "

Matt was deeply worried. At first the little medico had been mildly surprised at the seeming coincidence of five unconnected cases of food poisoning, Matt knew. Then he had discovered that all the sick men had eaten dinner together at Bedino's eating place several days before. He was puzzled for a while. He couldn't understand why, if they had eaten some contaminated food, it had taken so long for the results to show up. Then the high fever had appeared, along with the nausea, and he had immediately taken alarm.

He confided his troubles to Matt. He needed a place to isolate them and he wanted to keep the thing quiet until he was sure. Matt offered to let him use the block of jail cells, which fortunately was currently totally vacant. Doc moved the patients in under cover of darkness. He needed someone to nurse the men, so Matt appealed to Kitty Russell. She had assented promptly. Somewhat to Matt's surprise, she had been able to persuade Big Elsie, one of the Long Branch's favorite entertainers, a tall girl with bountiful physical attributes, to come along and help her. You never really knew people, Matt had reflected, until something big in the line of trouble developed.

Now, armed with a court order, secured on the application of Abe Botkin supported by Dr. Adams's affidavit, he could go into action himself. Up to now, he had been operating as Doc's ally and errand boy. Even this was somewhat foreign to his usual duties, but it was law work, of a kind. Taking Chester with him, he set out for Bedino's place.

They found the building that housed the restaurant darkened. There was nothing surprising in that; Bedino generally closed fairly early. Bedino lived in a couple of rooms in the rear of the building. There was no sign of a light there, either.

"Maybe he's took sick himself," Chester ventured.

"More likely he's just gone to bed," Matt said. "He opens up early mornings."

"What'll we do, then—come back in the mornin'?"

"Better get it over with now," Matt said. "No sense in letting him beat us out of bed, maybe, and start getting things ready for his breakfast business. We'll go wake him up, break the bad news, and put a padlock on the front door."

He tried the door. It was on the latch. He opened it wide and they went in. The sight revealed to them by the dim moonlight entering by window and open door stopped them in their tracks.

Some of the tables were overturned. Smashed chairs and shattered dishes lay on the floor. For a few moments they stood there in a silence accentuated by the ticking of a clock that sat on one end of the lunch counter.

"Lordy," Chester breathed. "It sure looks like Mather wasn't fooling none."

"Find a lamp somewhere," Matt said tightly.

He moved about slowly as Chester struck a match to start his search. Skirting one overturned table, he saw another beyond it that he hadn't noticed before. It looked too small for a table. It took the shape of a man's torso and legs. He hurriedly lit a match of his own and bent over.

The restaurant owner lay sprawled on his back. The wavering matchlight played over his face. His eyes were open wide, staring sightlessly at the ceiling.

"Never mind, Chester," Matt called.

"What is it?" Chester asked, and came slowly toward Matt.

"It's Bedino." Matt let his match flicker out and dropped it. "I don't need a lamp now. *He* never will."

"What do we do now?" Chester said after a minute of silence.

"I go looking for Mather," Matt said. He stayed there in his kneeling position for a while, one fist clenched. When he slowly rose to his feet he thought he had never felt wearier in his life.

He went to Kyle Mather's gambling hall. Fortunately Mather was alone in his private office when Matt got there. He seemed surprised that Matt should see fit to arrest him for what had happened. He tried to argue the marshal out of it but he didn't make any gun trouble.

"I tell you you're wastin' your time, Dillon," he insisted.

"The man was killed; you'll have to stand trial."

"No jury'll convict me when they know the facts of all this," Mather asserted. "Bedino shouldn't have tried to stand up to me and my boys."

"No use talking," Matt told him. "I'm taking you to jail. Hand over your gun."

When they reached the marshal's office they found Doc there, talking to Kitty. She looked haggard and drawn. When he heard what had happened, Doc turned on Mather in fury.

"You murdering fool! I had questions I wanted to ask Bedino! What those men ate. Where he got the food. Other things. Now I'll never know!"

"Don't yell at me!" the gambler lashed back at him. "If he'd been reasonable he wouldn't 'a' got hurt. I was doin' the town a favor; nobody knew for sure if Botkin could get that court order."

"You couldn't wait for the law, eh?" He turned disgustedly away from Mather and said to Matt, "Well, Richter's taken care of. Luckily I'm coroner as well as attending physician, so there'll be no trouble about that. I suppose I ought to go and view Bedino's body."

"No hurry about it," Matt said. "Chester's over there; he'll see that nobody else comes in."

"Kitty held the fort while I was away," Doc told him. "Nobody seems to be any worse."

"I sent Big Elsie back to the Long Branch," Kitty said. "If both of us stayed away all night people might start wondering."

A soft groan sounded from the cell block. Doc glanced that way.

"It's that Linden boy," Kitty said. "He's been calling for his mother. I'll go see to him." She turned away.

Doc watched her go, his face softening. "A good nurse has to be all things to all men. . . . Well, let's have some coffee."

There was a pot on the little stove in the office. Doc picked it up and started to pour a cup.

"Wait'll I salt Mather away, then I'll join you," Matt said.

They heard a faint knock at the door. Doc looked at Matt, put his cup down, and went over to open it. A middle-aged woman with a shawl around her shoulders stood there. Matt recognized her; she was the wife of Fred Sauer, a farmer with a place a few miles outside of Dodge. She leaned against the door jamb, obviously weak.

Doc extended his hand to her. "What is it, Mrs. Sauer?"

"Somebody said you was here, Doctor," she said in a faint voice. "I hitched up the wagon . . . drove in from our place lookin' for you."

Doc took her arm, led her to a chair. "Sit down here, ma'am," he said. "Where's Fred, anyway?"

"Him and the boy went way over to Morrison's fer somethin'," she told him. "They wasn't comin' home till mornin'."

"You're ill, Mrs. Sauer?"

"I feel so sick an' weak . . . oh I don't know what's wrong with me, Doctor . . ."

Having hastily taken her pulse, he put a hand on her brow and looked closely at her eyes. "Little fever, all right." He glanced at Matt and nodded slightly. "Bring my bag, will you, Kitty?" he called. "Now listen to me carefully, Mrs. Sauer." The woman nodded, closing her eyes.

"Have you eaten any food in Bedino's restaurant lately?" She shook her head.

"You sure you know the place I mean, Bedino's, over on Front Street?"

"I ain't even been to Dodge fer two months or more."

Matt looked at Kyle Mather. The gambler met his eyes, then nervously shifted his gaze.

Doc nodded grimly and came over to them. "Looks like it *was* just a coincidence, those five eating there at the same time," he said in a low voice.

"A good night's work," Matt said bitterly to Mather. "There was no reason at all for what you did . . ."

Mather cursed. "Why did the fool have to put up a fight?"

Doc, having been handed his bag by Kitty, had it open and was rummaging in it, talking to Mrs. Sauer as he did so. Matt took the gambler's arm.

"In we go," he said. "We'll move the man that was in the cell with Richter out into the corridor."

Mather sounded panicky. "Look, you can't put me back there with *them!*"

"Get moving," Matt said grimly.

When the shift had been made and he had left Mather standing tense and frightened in a locked cell, Matt came back into the office.

"What about her, Doc?" he said, indicating the ill woman.

Adams was closing his bag. "You stay here with her while I go over to Bedino's," he said. "I'll tell Chester to come and drive her home. From now on I'll isolate the cases where they occur—and hope for the best."

"She picked it up twelve miles out on the prairie, Doc?" Matt asked curiously.

"It looks that way," Doc replied. "Lord knows how many others have got it," he added tiredly. "Or how they got it."

Twenty-four hours later Doc and Matt had eleven cases

logged, and another one of the original five patients had died. In spite of their efforts, some garbled information had made the rounds. A good many people were getting uneasy and curious. Matt was about to enter his office when a gaunt, heavily bearded man hurried up to intercept him.

"Hey, Marshal!"

Matt turned. "Howdy, Dawson." He saw that the man was extremely agitated. "What's on your mind?"

"Say, I heard Doc Adams has got a lot o' sick fellers cached here in the jail."

"That's right," Matt admitted.

"They say Hank Schiller was one of 'em, and he jest died today."

"That's true, too," Matt said calmly.

"Well, what in the devil is wrong with 'em? What ha' they got?"

"Seems to be a rash of food poisoning; anyway, that's what the paper says."

"But why's the Doc got 'em roped off here like this?" Dawson persisted.

"Well, Doc's only one man, and he's got an overload of cases," Matt said. "It was handy for him to put 'em in here."

He turned away. Dawson tried to grasp his arm but Matt eluded him, stepped inside, and shut the door in the man's face. Dawson stood there for a moment, red-faced and angry, and then went away.

Kitty was still on duty, drooping a little with fatigue, but she summoned up a small smile for Matt.

"When Chester gets back from the Schiller place," he said gently, "you better go get some sleep. You're wearing yourself out."

"I'm all right," she told him. "Just call me Florence Nightingale."

"I figure even Florence grabbed a few winks now and then," Matt said, patting her arm. "I'm going over and see if Doc's in his office. Don't forget what I said now, if Chester comes in before I get back."

"Okay, boss," she said as he went out.

The light was on in Doc's office but no one was there. Matt rolled a cigarette and slumped down on the bench in front of the place. He had just finished it and flipped the stub away when Doc's buggy rolled down the street and stopped. Doc was singing in an off-key voice and swaying perilously on the seat. Matt jumped up and hurried out to the rig. Doc wrapped the lines around the whip socket and peered at him foolishly.

"You're drunk," Matt said quietly.

"My boy, you're a diagnostician," Doc said, having some trouble getting the word out. He groped for his bag, got it, and hopped awkwardly out of the buggy.

Matt caught him under one arm. "Doc, this isn't like you."

Doc drew himself up. "Ne' mind all the talk; I've got work to do."

Matt took time to loosen the horse's reins and hitch it to the rack before he followed the medico into the building. Doc had slipped out of his coat. He dropped it on the floor.

"Gotta cut a couple more notches in m' stethoscope," he muttered. "Blame bugs took two more patients t'day."

"All the more reason for you to stay sober," Matt told him.

"Know what I'm labelin' it now?" Doc demanded, looking blearily at the marshal. " 'Intestinal complications,' 'f you please!" He took a lurching step toward his desk.

"Take it easy, Doc," Matt said.

Doc swung around and glared at him. "Know where I come from just now? Meetin' with a committee of virtuous, civic-minded citizens!" he announced loudly.

Matt closed the door quickly. "All right, tell me about it."

Doc pushed a pile of opened medical books and periodicals off the desk top and set his bag down. "I'll tell you what those self-righteous pups did! They practically threatened to lynch me if I said anything in public about an epidemic! They'd brand me a liar, they'd ride me out of town on a rail, they'd . . ."

"Easy, Doc." Matt pleaded.

"Let me add," he went on, "that our Mr. Botkin and some of the others have sent their families to Topeka!"

He bent over and picked up a book from the floor. "Sewers leaking into the Thames . . . bugs in the water . . . so they get typhoid . . ." He threw the book down again. "No sewers around here, Matt." Tears came into his eyes. "I'm stuck, Matt . . . beat . . ." He let the tears roll down his face; his shoulders started to shake and he sobbed.

There was a pitcher of water on a washstand in a corner of the room. Matt grabbed it and emptied it over the weeping man's head. He gasped, raised his head and glared at Matt, sputtering, then he sat down in the chair behind his desk, got out a kerchief and wiped his face.

"Well, that was quite a demonstration," he said. "You're an officer, though, and a conscientious one, so you can understand. You can't live with yourself when you're only doing half a job."

Matt took a sheet of paper from his pocket and put it down on the desk top. "Tell me what you think of this idea of mine." Doc leaned over to squint at it. "This is a list of all the ones that have come down with the typhoid so far. Can you read it? . . . The names are all German—every one."

Doc looked at him quickly. "So were the two new ones today—Lindlahr and Kuhn."

"Remember the first five?" Matt prodded. "They were at Bedino's—making plans for the German picnic."

Doc rose to his feet. "Lord, yes—the picnic!"

"Could be *all* these people were there, coming from miles around."

Doc gripped his shoulder. "Matt, maybe you've put your finger on it!" He picked his coat off the floor. "Let's go."

"Where to?"

"The jail. I want to talk to those patients we've still got over there."

A few minutes later, they were sitting next to the cot where Alex Berkleman lay. He listened while Doc read him the names from the list Matt had written down. When he had finished the pudgy German thought for a minute.

"*Ja,*" he said finally. "They was all there, Doctor; I'm sure of it."

"What about the food you had to eat?" Doc pressed.

"*Schlachtfest,*" Berkleman said. "Pork feast, it means. We ate nothing but pork, just like we do every year. Pork cooked all kinds of ways."

"Who was the cook?" Doc was crumpling the list in his hands.

"Franz Pelzer."

"Pelzer the blacksmith?" Matt asked, surprised.

"Sure," Berkleman said weakly. "Franz was a fine chef, in the old country."

Doc stood up slowly. "Thanks, Alex. Thanks very much."

Matt followed him out of the cell. "Pelzer the next stop, Doc?"

"Come on!" was Doc's only answer.

They had to get Pelzer out of bed to answer the door. After he let them in, he sat on the edge of his rude cot, a red-faced, fleshy man, his hairy chest showing through the gaps in his long underwear. He listened as Doc talked, a frown building on his heavy features. When Doc finished, he turned to Matt, his face wrathful.

"What is this, Herr Marshal?" he demanded in a thick voice. "What is he saying to me?"

"You heard him, Pelzer," Matt said.

"*Ja,*" he said. "*Ja,* I heard *und* I don't like what I heard!" He swung his huge head back at Doc. "You are saying my food makes people sick! But I am saying you are wrong, Herr Doktor! Back in Pilsen a chef I was! No woman cooks as good as me!"

"All right, all right," Doc said. "You're a good cook, Franz. Where'd you get the pork you used?"

"At Peter Schrafft's farm," Pelzer answered, somewhat appeased. "Fresh-killed, it was. I was there . . . I dressed it myself, mit my own hands." He held out his huge paws.

Doc looked at him and frowned. "Have you been feeling a little feverish lately, maybe?" he said, hopefully.

"Hah! I never felt more good in my life!" Pelzer exploded again. "*Und* I eat more sausage than anybody. All der spices I used, *und* I had to make it just right, so I tasted *und* tasted!" He sat up straight and thrust out his great chest. "I look sick, maybe? Go ahead, Doktor, examine me! Nobody is stronger than Pelzer."

Doc shook his head, smiling a little. "No need for that; you look fine, Franz." His voice went lower. "Look, Franz, let's be friends, eh?"

The German shrugged. "Everybody is Franz Pelzer's friend . . ."

"All right, then," Doc said, "how about cooking a batch of sausage for me tomorrow? Right here on your own stove?"

Pelzer looked at him suspiciously. "A joke you are making, Doktor?"

"No, Franz, I mean it. I'll go out to Schrafft's and pick up the pork myself."

Pelzer shrugged again. "Sure, I do it," he said. "I make you some sausage—goot sausage."

"Fine!" Doc got up. "We'll be here around twelve o'clock. If you don't mind, we'll bring a young lady with us."

The German looked puzzled but gave his assent. Doc and Matt went out. When they were outside, Matt said: " 'Young lady'? Who'll that be, Doc?"

"Kitty Russell," Doc said. When Matt looked a further question at him, he added, "Pelzer is going to cook sausage for *me*. Kitty's going to cook some for *you*."

Matt couldn't make him say what he was up to.

The next day at noon they were in Franz Pelzer's big kitchen. Doc had brought in the pork from Schrafft's farm, as promised. Matt was there, and so were Kitty and Chester. Big Elsie was on duty at the jail-infirmary.

Franz Pelzer was happy when they set him to work grinding and kneading the sausage meat. His smile changed to a look of bewilderment when Doc set Kitty to work on another batch of the pork. Matt watched it all with interest. Chester looked on, as puzzled as the ponderous German. Pelzer, watching Kitty frowningly, decided he wanted to help her. She wasn't getting enough seasoning into her batch, any *dummkopf* could see that. He started to remedy the lack. Doc caught him in time, made him desist. He glowered at Kitty until she smiled at him timidly and spread her hands, then he went back to his own kneading. Anyway, he'd show these *Amerikaners* who knew how to make the best sausage. . . .

When they had the meat prepared, Doc had Pelzer cook four sausages made from his batch in one skillet, Kitty four from hers in another. Pelzer fussed over his, his huge frame hovering above the hot stove, on ludicrous tiptoes. Kitty handled her skillet matter-of-factly on the other side of the big old wood-burner. The German leaned over and sniffed the aroma rising from his sausages, his fat face registering deep satisfaction. Then he glanced at Kitty's skillet and his face hardened.

Her eyebrows went up. She caught Matt grinning at her and she winked at him surreptitiously. Bending over her own skillet, she took a deep breath and let a beatific smile show on her face. Matt chuckled. She beamed over at the scowling Pelzer.

When the sausages were done, Doc had Matt sit down at the table. He placed the ones Kitty had prepared on a plate in front of the marshal. Then he ladled some out of Pelzer's skillet onto another plate and went to the other side of the table with it.

"Sorry, folks," he said to the others. "This has got to be a private *schlachtfest*. Are you ready, Marshal?"

Matt started to pick up a fork, then changed his mind. He put the fork down, got to his feet, and went part way around the table.

"I move we call this off," he said.

"What's the matter?" Doc said chidingly. "Afraid of Kitty's cooking?"

"I've got a feeling this thing could cost us a doctor, that's all," Matt said quietly; "and we can't afford to lose one."

Pelzer was staring at them, open-mouthed. "Gentlemen, what iss this? Please, you are going to eat my goot sausages?"

"Yeah, what you arguin' about, anyhow?" It was Chester's voice, coming from near the stove. "This here sausage the Dutchman cooked is right tasty!"

Matt and Doc swung around simultaneously. Chester was standing by the stove. He had just finished swallowing. He was spearing the fork he held into another portion of sausage left in Pelzer's skillet.

Doc fairly leaped at him. He grabbed the skillet, knocked the fork out of Chester's hand. Chester stared at him as if he were out of his mind.

"What's the matter with you?" he demanded. "There was some left here, and I was only—"

"Oh shut up!" Doc barked at him. He turned and said to Kitty, "You and Chester take a little walk outside, will you?"

She didn't understand this any more than Chester did, but she nodded to Doc and head-gestured at Chester. His face still a mystified mask, the deputy followed her out the door.

"You too, Franz," Doc said Pelzer. "I want to talk to the marshal alone."

The German looked at them, his face red. He started to say something, and then decided against it. He was clearly dealing with unbalanced people. He sighed heavily and went out.

Matt looked at Doc. "Well, are you going to let me in on it now?"

"Sure," Doc said. He brushed past Matt, sat down at the table, and calmly started to eat the sausages Kitty had fixed. "I'll gladly let you in on it, *now*. Until you interfered, in your high-handed way, I was conducting a controlled scientific experiment."

"Then what are you doing now?"

"I'm eating the food Kitty cooked, since Chester helped himself to what Franz cooked."

Matt looked at him. "So whatever you expected might happen to you may now happen to Chester?"

"Exactly," Doc said. "If I'm right in my guess, Chester will get typhoid, and nothing will happen to me."

"Figured it was like that."

Doc chewed another mouthful and swallowed it. "At first I was sure it must be the food those people ate at the picnic. But this big hulk of a Franz said he ate more than anybody else there, and looking at him, I had to believe him. He was still walking around, sound and healthy. So I had a sudden hunch."

"What d'you mean, Doc?"

"There's nothing like it in the medical literature, or at least I haven't seen it if there is. But maybe—just maybe— Franz Pelzer carries the bug around with him. He prepares food, other people eat it—and bang!"

"But why wouldn't he get it himself?"

"I don't know, Matt. Somehow he's got a natural protection against it, within his own body. He takes it around with him but it never makes *him* sick. That's a guess, no more."

"So if Chester comes down with it, you'll be sure what caused the epidemic?"

"That's it," Doc said gravely. "To prove my point, Chester has to get sick. Maybe die."

All they could do after that was wait. Doc would have liked to spend all his time watching Chester, but he couldn't afford to. Several more cases turned up, all among the Germans in and around Dodge who had attended what Doc was now privately thinking of as the fatal picnic; and there were two more deaths. It all made a heavy and wearisome task, added to his usual rounds, but he maintained a pace and a light-hearted manner that continually surprised Matt.

One day, right after Doc had gone over Chester painstakingly and found nothing wrong. Matt was talking to the medico when Abe Botkin bustled in. He was beaming; he bore good news, he thought.

"Came over to tell you that you win, Doctor," he announced. "People have been talking plague and they're beginning to get frightened. We've decided to send a telegram to the Governor."

"Now hold on," Doc remonstrated, as Botkin, who was already on his way out, looked back at him inquiringly. "This time *I'm* asking for a few days."

"By your own report, we've got eighteen cases now!" Botkin exclaimed. "Can you say that the end is in sight, Doctor?"

"I'm waiting for the outcome of one particular case," Doc told him. "If it comes out the way I think it will, I'll be able to give Dodge a clean bill of health."

With Matt adding his plea to Doc's, Botkin finally agreed to hold off for another day. The added twenty-four hours were enough. The next morning Matt suddenly realized that Chester had been wiping his forehead a great deal. When the deputy wondered aloud why he'd been feeling so doggone thirsty all morning, Matt hot-footed it to Doc's office.

"Come on!" he said, sticking his head through the doorway. "Something's wrong with Chester!"

When they got back to the marshal's office, they found Chester sprawled on the floor.

That was the beginning of the end. They let Botkin in on it all, and he postponed indefinitely the sending of the appeal to the Governor. A public announcement appeared on the front page of *Dodge City Times*, as Matt had asked, quoting Doc Adams to the effect that the epidemic was under control and that anyone who skinned out of Dodge on account of it was a triple-dyed fool.

Matt read it through. "What d'you mean, Doc: 'under control'?"

"I mean Pelzer," Doc answered. "As long as he doesn't touch any food that people put in their mouths, we won't have any problem."

"Did you make him understand that?" Matt said.

"I had a real heart-to-heart talk with Franz," Doc answered. He gave a little chuckle. "When I was through he was so scared he swore he wasn't going to cook for himself, even."

"Any idea where *he* could have picked up the bug?"

"Well, he was in Kansas City not long ago, visiting a sister of his. He probably got it there somehow. He doesn't know."

"All we've got to worry about now is Chester, I guess," Matt said.

"Don't worry; I think he'll pull through."

If care meant anything, Matt thought, Doc had to be right. With Matt and Kitty and Doc all deeply concerned, Chester got around-the-clock attention.

Less than twelve hours after Doc had made his optimistic prediction, Chester opened his eyes and, for the first time since he'd been put to bed, recognized Matt, who was standing anxiously beside the bed.

"Welcome back, Chester," Matt said with a wide grin of relief. "You left us kind of sudden, boy."

"I'm sure glad . . . to be back," Chester said weakly. He made an effort to raise himself up on one elbow.

Matt eased him back. "No hurry getting up," he said. "I expect you'll be a mite under the weather for a few days yet. I'll do my best to keep things under control till you get around again."

Chester smiled faintly. "Just le' me know if you need any help, Marshal." Then: "What in heck happened, anyway?"

"We can spell it all out later," Matt told him. "For now, we'll just say it was something you ate."

HICKOK

When Chester brought the telegram to Matt he said he didn't know what was in it. He was excited, though, so Matt guessed the deputy must have been told who the sender was when he'd gotten it from the telegrapher.

Matt glanced at it, then up at Chester. "From Bill Hickok," he said.

"Yeah," Chester said, confirmatively.

"I didn't know you knew, Chester," Matt commented innocently.

"What's he want?" Chester said, unembarrassed.

Matt grinned and read it aloud: *"Jack Teeters Tom Gridler reported heading for Dodge. They committed two murders here and were tried for one but we could not produce witnesses so they got off. Witness to other murder has now turned up and we want him to make identification before arrest. Hold them in Dodge till I get there with witness."*

"Hickok's comin' here from Abilene?" Chester asked when Matt had finished.

"Looks that way," Matt said, tossing the telegram on his desk.

"How you goin' to recognize them two?"

"I think I'll be able to recognize them, all right," Matt said, rubbing his chin.

"Sounds like you know the gents," Chester remarked.

"We have met," Matt admitted. "Briefly—and unofficially. The pair of them have been partners in sin for quite some time. They're not very bright—but that may make them all the more dangerous. They hold human life cheaply not because they're calculating and callous, but because they are unthinking and brutal."

"You mean they don't know no better, Marshal?"

"Thank you, Chester," Matt said; "you've put my thought clearly and simply." He leaned back in his chair. "I suppose we'd better start meeting the trains. Teeters and Gridler will be coming in."

"One gets in at noon," Chester said. "You goin' to clap 'em into the *juzgado,* Marshal?"

"I'm afraid we can't do anything as bold and direct as that," Matt told him. "Bill said he wants his witness to identify them before the arrest, remember?"

"Oh yeah—'hold' 'em, he said. How you goin' to hold 'em without arrestin' 'em?" Chester looked vaguely worried.

"I'm not sure, Chester. Maybe I'm supposed to do it by the sheer force of my personality," Matt said sourly.

The westbound was running a little late. Matt and Chester lounged near the depot, as inconspicuously as possible. The marshal exhaled smoke from his cigarette and studied it as it drifted slowly away on the still air. He didn't have much of a plan for handling this. If the two wanted men got off at Dodge he could keep them under surveillance, that was about all. Teeters and Gridler were dangerous, but they weren't likely to give him any trouble as long as they didn't get the idea that he was especially interested in them. They knew that he knew them, though, so if he ignored them that in itself might make them spooky. Men of their stripe weren't used to being ignored—didn't like being ignored, probably. . . .

He hadn't seen Hickok for quite a while. He'd always gotten along well enough with Bill, even if he didn't admire him as much as a good many people did, or pretended they did. Hickok mixed gambling with his law work. That wasn't an important thing in itself; but Bill was a quick trigger, up to the point of being nervous. Matt knew that once, in a tight situation, the Abilene marshal had made a quick-turning snap shot—and put a bullet in his own deputy. . . .

Well, every lawman had his own methods. His own strengths and his own weaknesses. You didn't go around criticizing a fellow officer who was on top of his job. Matt took a last drag on his smoke and snuffed it out.

The train was coming in. Matt and Chester watched as it hissed and clanked to a stop. Passengers alighted. Matt spotted the ones they were looking for.

"Getting off the end car, Chester," he said conversationally. "The tall one in the black hat is Jack Teeters. The other is Tom Gridler. Let's ease around the corner here and see where they head for."

They did so. In a moment Teeters and Gridler appeared and set off purposefully, Gridler taking quick steps to keep pace with the long-striding man in the black hat.

"Goin' to the Dodge House, looks like," Chester said.

"Yeah. Wait a minute, then we'll follow along."

Matt and the deputy were some fifty yards back when the two men entered the hotel. The marshal halted.

"Let's wait here a minute. I'll give them time to get a room and then I'll go in and talk to them."

"Now why should you do that?" Chester asked plaintively. "If you don't mean to arrest 'em. . . ?"

"I kind of think they expect it, Chester. So I might as well do it now as later. But I want you to go back to the depot and ask George Bishop to let me know if Teeters and Gridler come down there to take a train any time. You can describe them for him."

"All right," Chester said.

"And then go to the stage office and do the same. Cover the stables, too. If they rent any horses, or buy any, I want to know about it right off."

Chester started away. "Tell them to keep quiet about it, though," Matt called after him. "See you later, at the office."

He walked to the Dodge House and entered the lobby. Giff Orchard was at the desk. Matt greeted him, and Orchard responded warmly. He was a young man and seemed eager to co-operate with the law whenever he had a chance. Matt told him he'd seen the two men, one wearing a black hat, come in a few minutes earlier.

Orchard nodded. "They took a room here, Marshal."

"I know them," Matt said. "Their names are Teeters and Gridler. Did they register that way?"

Orchard said they had. "The tall one signed for both of them," he commented. "They look like hardcases to me."

"You have a good eye," Matt told him. "What's their room number?"

"Twenty-five," Orchard responded. He hesitated, then: "Uh, Marshal, if you want to arrest them, couldn't you wait till they go out?"

"I know your walls are thin," Matt said, grinning, "but there's likely to be more people who might get hit by a stray bullet out on the street than there is in here." He held up a hand as the clerk opened his mouth. "Don't worry, though, I'm just aiming to talk to 'em."

Orchard relaxed visibly. "All right, Marshal. Up the stairs and turn left."

Matt thanked him and climbed the stairs. He walked down
the hall, located Number 25, and knocked on the door.

"Who's there?" someone called from within.

Matt knocked again.

"I said who's there?" the voice said, more loudly. After a
short, silent wait, it said: "Open it up, Tom."

Matt heard the bolt being drawn back. The door opened.
Tom Gridler stood there, a gun in his hand, a scowl on his
heavy, square face.

"Put it away, Gridler," Matt said. "I just came up for a
little talk."

Gridler squinted at him. Matt couldn't be sure whether the
man recognized him or not. "Make your talk, then," Gridler
said.

Jack Teeters towered into view behind him, his black hat
still riding on his rusty-colored hair. "You ain't bein' polite,
Tom," he said. "Let Marshal Dillon in." He grinned crooked-
ly. "We can watch him better inside anyways."

Gridler stood there for a moment, then grunted, holstered
his gun, and stepped aside. Matt went in and closed the door
behind him.

"Howdy, Teeters," he said.

The tall man slouched down on the double bed while Gridler moved over near the window, keeping his gaze on Matt.

"What's on your mind, Dillon?"

"Haven't seen you boys for quite a while," Matt said easily.
"Where was it, now—Tascosa?"

"What's this all about?" Gridler growled.

"I know you're a friendly cuss, Marshal," Teeters said, "but
I doubt if you come up here to pass the time o' day."

"No cause for you to be edgy," Matt said. "Heard you
boys were in town so I thought I better say hello."

Gridler spat on the floor. "News gits around purty fast in
Dodge."

"Mebbe he was expectin' us, Tom," Jack Teeters said.

"Well, I happened to see you get off the train," Matt said,
"and when I dropped in here I found out you were
registered."

"Nothin' wrong with that, is there?" Teeters said coolly.
"Nobody's lookin' for us, I can tell you that." He narrowed
his eyes at Matt. "We had a little trouble in Abilene but the
judge up there done turned us loose."

"That danged Hickok tried to frame us," Gridler said venomously.

"And it didn't work," Teeters finished, with a little smile. "So what d'you want, now?"

"Just this, boys," Matt said gravely. "You know me. You know I'm still the law here in Dodge. I want you both to get this—that there's to be no trouble from you while you're here."

"Heck, we're not lookin' for trouble," Teeters answered.

Matt managed a small sigh and let his body relax. "That's fine, then. Boys, you're welcome to stay as long as you like, on those terms."

Teeters looked at him, not quite satisfied. "That's a kinda funny thing for you to tell us," he said.

"You know this is an open town," Matt told him.

"Well, sure," Teeters said. "Sure, we know it's that, Marshal." He sounded a bit friendlier.

"Anybody starts any trouble, it won't be us," Gridler rumbled.

"As long as you keep it that way, the town's yours," Matt said.

"I figgered you'd spot us quick enough," Teeters remarked, "but durn if I thought you'd be around to give us the keys to the city." He glanced at Gridler. "Let's git a clean shirt on and make the rounds, Tom. This ain't likely to last forever."

Matt grinned and opened the door to leave. "Some pretty sharp gamblers around here," he said lightly; "watch out they don't relieve you of all your money."

"Don't let it worry you none, Marshal," Teeters said.

Matt went out and down the stairs. He guessed he'd put it over all right. If the two of them decided to do some gambling, and if their money held out, they might hang around Dodge for a week. If Teeters' apparent assurance was only simulated, however, they might pull stakes and leave town within the hour.

He kept close tabs on them. They dropped into several saloons and had at least one drink in each. Then they got something to eat and afterward settled down in the Alafraganza, bucking faro. Matt decided they meant to stay on for some time. All he could do now was hope they didn't get into a fight over the cards and leave in a hurry.

At ten o'clock that evening he was at his office desk when Chester hurried in. Matt asked him what was up.

"They're fixin' to leave, Marshal, early in the mornin'!"

Matt fixed a questioning eye on his deputy.

"Jim Bunch, over at the stage office, just told me they come in and bought tickets to Sharon Springs and asked him what time the stage left in the mornin'."

"Sharon Springs . . ." Matt echoed. "Guess they're heading for Denver." He pulled at his under lip. "Go tell Jim Bunch that I'll be on the stage in the morning, too. I'll ride shotgun for him if he wants me to. His regular man can take the day off."

"All right," Chester said dubiously. "You goin' all the way up to Denver?"

"If I have to, I'll follow them to San Francisco. Tell Hickok when he shows up."

"Too bad he won't get here before they leave," Chester said.

"Another day before he could make it. But that won't leave him too far behind. The stage leaves at eight, doesn't it?"

The stage for Sharon Springs and Denver did leave at eight the following morning, but it left without Marshal Matt Dillon. He stayed in Dodge City because Jack Teeters and Tom Gridler failed to show up at the stage depot and it pulled out with just one passenger aboard, a gaunt Lutheran minister who seemed glad to be saying farewell to Dodge. The regular shotgun guard had already started to enjoy an unexpected holiday but Jim Bunch came up with a replacement quickly and there was no delay.

Disgusted, Matt had watched the stage pull out of sight. Now he turned to head for the Dodge House. He wanted to check on Teeters and Gridler and see what they were up to. He had taken not more than a dozen steps when he sighted them riding down the street.

Chester, beside him, touched his arm and said, "Look."

"I see 'em," Matt said grimly. "I wonder what their game is."

"That stage-ticket thing was a pure fraud," Chester said bitterly.

"Well, they might have aimed to go on it and then changed

their minds," Matt said, "though I doubt it. They can always use those tickets later—or turn them in."

The pair of hardcases drew near them. Teeters reined his horse down to a slow walk and raised a hand. He grinned slyly at Matt.

"Up early, ain't you, Marshal?" he asked.

"Yeah," Matt said, a trifle sourly. "So are you, for that matter."

"It's cooler in the mornin', and I like that," Teeters said. "Specially to travel by."

"What happened, did you boys lose all your money last night?" Matt was trying hard to keep his composure.

"That was good advice you give us," the tall man said. "We'll follow it, next time. There's nothin' left for us in Dodge now, though." He touched his horse with the spurs and flipped a hand at Matt and Chester. Tom Gridler followed suit, without as much as looking at them.

"We goin' after 'em?" Chester demanded.

"I am," Matt said. "You stay here and give Hickok the low-down when he pulls in. I'll saddle up and get on their trail as soon as they're well out of sight. I'll leave as clear a trail as I can for Bill."

He put in a long and, as it turned out, profitless day's ride. He tried to stay out of the two men's sight, although there was no doubt that if they suspected they might be followed they could have confirmed their suspicions without any trouble. They traversed long stretches of powder-dry ground that marked their horses' passage, and his too, with persistent dust clouds.

What they did was to pass the day by riding in a great half-circle, coming back into Dodge shortly after sundown from the direction opposite to that in which they had ridden out in the morning. Matt was sure that was what they were doing within two hours after the long, leisurely chase began, but he did not dare take the chance of returning directly to Dodge ahead of them, for fear that they would see the telltale cloud of dust he'd raise and, assuming that they knew it was he, then might head off in another direction in an effort to shake him.

As it was, the laugh was on him. He waited outside of town a couple of miles and then rode in after full dark. He put up his horse and gave him a feed of grain. No one was at the office. He walked to Delmonico's and found Doc

Adams having a late supper there. Doc waved him over, and Matt sat down glumly.

"You do look hungry, son," Doc said, inspecting him curiously. "Shall I order you *two* steaks?"

"Don't think I couldn't eat 'em," Matt said wearily. "It's been a mighty long time since breakfast."

"Sounds like you had a hard day," Doc observed.

"Yeah," Matt said. "Riding all day. In circles, at that."

"What happened?" Doc asked casually. "You lose 'em?"

Matt raised his eyes. "I have sources of information, my boy," Doc told him.

"Does the source walk upright like a human being and answer to the name of Chester?" Matt asked drily.

Doc nodded, then said hastily, "Don't get mad, now; there was no harm in it."

The glint went out of Matt's eyes. "No, I didn't lose 'em," he said. His gaze swung to the doorway. "As a matter of fact, here they come right now."

Doc followed his glance. "Hard-looking pair," he murmured.

Matt watched the two, still dust-covered, as they tramped over to the table where he and Doc sat. The shorter man's habitual glower darkened Gridler's features, but Teeters was maintaining a poker face as they halted a few feet away.

"Evenin', Marshal," he said.

"Well, boys," Matt returned. "This is Doc Adams. Teeters ... Gridler."

Teeters said howdy and the heavy man grunted.

"What's on your mind?" Matt asked after a moment's silence.

"I reckon you are, Marshal," Teeters said softly.

"Yeah?" Matt said, sitting up straighter.

"That was you trailin' us all day, wasn't it." The way Teeters said it, it was not a question.

There wouldn't be much point in denying it, Matt knew. "Yes, it was," he said. He was watching both of them now.

"Mind tellin' us why?" Teeters prodded.

"Maybe I didn't want you to get lost," Matt said, with some measure of truth. They did not respond to that, so he added, "Remember, I told you I didn't want you to get into any trouble."

Teeters shoved his hat back with his thumb. "That sounds like a lot of bull to me, Marshal."

"Look," Matt said, "you boys' reputations aren't of the best. My job is to preserve the peace in this neck of the woods. I decided I'd keep an eye on you, that's all."

"Man, you sure been doin' that," Teeters retorted.

"Well, I hope we understand each other now," Matt said. "But it's as I told you—keep out of trouble and stay as long as you want."

Gridler spoke for the first time. "Remember one thing," he said hoarsely. "There's two of us."

"Yeah." Teeters' face was cold and hard. "Hound-dog us agin, and might be you won't come back."

"I get paid for taking chances," Matt said calmly.

Gridler looked at his partner. "Come on," he growled, "let's git outa here."

"Sure," Teeters said, and without any more talk they went out.

"Talk a little rough, don't they?" Doc said soberly.

Matt was looking after them musingly. "I guess they're a little smarter than I figured," he said. "Or Teeters is anyway. I thought I had him fooled yesterday, but he must sense that something is wrong, even if he doesn't know what."

"Think they might bolt?"

"Depends on how smart they really are. I don't think they will, though. More likely, they'll be so curious now that they'll stick around just to find out what it's all about."

After he had eaten, Matt dropped in at the Dodge House. He found out that Teeters and Gridler were still in Number 25. In fact, the clerk told him, they had never checked out. Matt felt like kicking himself. He had spent the day tipping his hand to them. Fortunately, they still hadn't gotten a peek at his hole card. To men of their stamp, that would be pretty much of a challenge. He had to count on that.

The pair did no gambling that night, but apparently they still had money in their jeans; they visited two or three places, spending all their time at the bar. When they went back to the Dodge House and, ostensibly, to bed, Matt was ready for some rest himself.

They were still in town the next morning. Having ascertained that, Matt went to the railroad station to meet the train from Abilene. Hickok did not get off. Matt located the conductor, who told him that Hickok had ridden the whole way in the baggage car and that the Abilene lawman had someone with him. As soon as the crowd left the depot, Matt went to the other side of the baggage car and pounded on the door.

"Who is it?" a voice called.

"It's Dillon," Matt answered. "Open up, Bill."

The door slid part way open and a hand was thrust forth. "Jump up, Matt." Hickok gave him a pull-up as he climbed into the car. "How are you?"

"Fine, Bill. And you?"

"Couldn't be better," Hickok said. "This is my witness, Sam Trimble."

Matt peered in the dusk of the car at the disheveled, worried-looking man who had accompanied Hickok. He extended his hand and Trimble touched it and mumbled an acknowledgment.

"They still here, Matt?" Hickok wanted to know.

"Yes, but we may have to move fast; they're spooky."

"Matt, I'll swear that judge back there's got it in for me." Hickok shook his head, and the long hair that Matt had always noted as an affectation swung back and forth. "But he's still the judge, and he says he wants an identification of Teeters and Gridler on this second murder charge before they're arrested. Trimble here was an eye witness and that's why I brought him with me."

"We ought to be able to manage it, then, Bill."

"I'd say the devil with it and let's just go out and kill the pair of them but I believe I'd get even more pleasure in seeing them hang."

"You will, if we're lucky." Matt turned to Trimble. "Do these men know you on sight?"

"Well, I tell you how it was," Trimble replied. "I was in this stable where I work, over in Abilene I mean, and a feller come in fer his horse and I went to git it fer him. Then I heard some shootin' an' two men run right past me but I got a good look at 'em, all right, they'd jest killed that feller, the one come in fer his horse."

"You mean you don't know the two men here, Teeters and Gridler?"

"He never heard of them, Matt," Hickok explained. "And there's no pictures of them that I know of. He can identify them when he sees them, though."

"All right," Matt said. "But what about them? Will they recognize you, Trimble?"

The man swung his head, looking at Hickok, then back at Matt. "Gosh, I dunno. I hope not . . . they'd kill me on sight if'n they did, wouldn't they?" He began to stammer. "I —I hadn't th-thought o' that."

"Now you just do what we tell you and you'll come to no harm, Sam," Hickok told him soothingly. "Matt here and I are a pretty good match for those two. I don't reckon they'll start any trouble with us but if they do they'll die on their feet."

It was the kind of bragging talk that one had to expect from Hickok, Matt knew. Not but what it was probably justified: Matt had confidence in himself and he judged that Bill was if anything better than himself. Still, it made him uneasy. And Hickok had apparently not given this simple fellow the slightest hint that the task of identifying the two gunmen might put him in danger of his own life.

"I'm afraid I'm takin' a awful chance, Mr. Hickok." He turned on the Abilene lawman, "I don't know if I oughta . . ."

"Easy now, Sam!" Hickok cut him off sharply. "There's no need for you to worry, I tell you. Why, in an hour we'll have them in jail, with their teeth pulled."

"I sure hope so," Trimble said in a small voice. "How you goin' to do it, Mr. Hickok?"

"We'll have to locate them first," Matt said. "I told Chester —he's my deputy—to meet us at the Long Branch, and slip us the word where they are. I didn't want the two of you to be seen around my office ahead of time."

"Good!" Hickok put his hand on Trimble's shoulder. "As soon as we get them locked up, I'll buy you the biggest steak you ever ate, Sam." He poked his head out the baggage car door and looked around. "Come on, boys, let's go."

They kept to the alleys and went into the Long Branch by the back door. It was still early in the afternoon and the place was almost deserted, but even so Matt got out in front and had Hickok stand nearest to the back wall of the place. The bartender came to them but before he took their order he recognized Hickok and opened his mouth in surprise. Matt made a quick silencing gesture and he closed it again.

"Bring us a bottle," Hickok said to him.

The idea was to bolster up Trimble, who seemed to be getting close to a funk. He grabbed the first drink that Hickok poured for him, his hand trembling, and tossed it down. Bill calmly refilled his glass.

"Take it easy, friend," he said. "Everything's going to be all right."

"Mr. Hickok," Trimble said in a low voice, "I wouldn't 'a' come if'n I'd thought about it, I jest wouldn't 'a'."

"Listen, Sam," Hickok told him solemnly, "it isn't often a man has my guns and Matt Dillon's both behind him. Why, you're as safe as if you was in church."

Trimble's eyes were round. "I—I don't go to church," he said self-accusingly. "I wish I did . . ." He downed his second drink, the sweat breaking out on his brow.

Hickok filled his glass again. He looked grimly at Matt, over the trembling man's lowered head. "A couple more ought to do it," he whispered. Trimble, immersed in his worries, did not hear him.

Chester came in, by the front door. He saw them and hurried back. Teeters and Gridler, he reported, had left the hotel, eaten dinner in a restaurant, dropped into a saloon for a while, and then gone back to the Dodge House, where they were now.

"They didn't stay in the lobby, did they, Chester?" Matt asked.

"No, they went right upstairs."

"Good," Hickok said. "We can sit in the lobby and wait for them to come down. Then Sam here can identify them."

"If he can still see," Matt answered. "Better take that stuff away from him, Bill. And you better keep out of sight yourself—if they spot you first they'll light a shuck before Trimble can get a good look at them." He turned to Chester. "You get back there quick as you can. I'll come over with Trimble while Bill goes around and sneaks in the back way. If they've come back down to the lobby, you come to the door and give me the high sign so we don't walk in on anything unprepared."

Chester set out. Trimble, however, put up an argument. He wasn't going to go *anywhere* without Matt and Hickok both alongside. Hickok tried to talk him out of it but he stubbornly refused to leave the Long Branch unless both the lawmen accompanied him.

Finally Hickok threw up his hands. "There's no help for it," he said to Matt. "We'll have to risk it and both go with him. Maybe he's right, anyway—if they remember him they may go for their guns and no mistake."

There was nothing else to do. Matt didn't like it, though. There wasn't much of a chance, it seemed to him, that the two would have got a good look at the stable helper in their hurry to clear out after the shooting. But they would certainly recognize Hickok as soon as they saw him, and then the fat would be in the fire for sure . . .

He managed to swallow his doubts. The two lawmen escorted Trimble out of the Long Branch and, ranged on either side of him, partly supporting him, they walked him toward the Dodge House.

As they approached the hotel, Matt scanned it anxiously. There was no sign of Chester. They got to the door. Matt opened it while Hickok held Trimble upright, his big left hand clutched around the stable helper's arm. Chester was in the lobby, alone except for the man behind the desk. The deputy shook his head in a negative. The two men had not showed up.

Matt held the door open and motioned to Hickok to bring Trimble in. Through the door they came, Hickok continuing to support the frightened man. He guided Trimble to one of the lobby chairs and eased him down into it. In a low voice he told Trimble to keep his eyes on the stairway. The stable helper didn't seem to hear him. Hickok repeated his words, sharply this time. The man nodded and focused his wide-eyed gaze on the stairs.

Hickok glanced at Matt in relief and Matt motioned him to take up a position in the corridor that led to the back entrance. Hickok turned to comply with the signal.

As he did so the sound of a footstep came from the head of the stairs and Matt saw Trimble's hands grip the arms of his chair. He swung his head and looked up. Jack Teeters had paused on the top step, from where he commanded a full view of the lobby, including the frightened Trimble, Matt standing near by, and Hickok, with his long, flowing hair conspicuous, about to turn into the corridor.

Matt saw Gridler crowding behind Teeters even as the tall gunman's right hand dipped and came up. He went for his own gun, calling a warning to Hickok as he did so. Teeters' gun flashed and boomed and Trimble lurched out of his chair with a strangled cry and fell into Matt. Hickok had whirled around and, his gun incredibly clear of leather already, flung a shot up the stairway. It chipped plaster from the wall a foot from Teeters. The tall gunman turned in a panic, pushed Gridler back, and they both disappeared from view.

Hickok started up the stairs. "No, Bill!" Matt shouted. "They'll go down the back stairs, try to make it out the back door!"

Hickok reversed and took off down the corridor to the rear, pulling out his second gun as he went, his long hair flying. Chester, his own gun out, started after him. Matt called him back.

"Watch the stairs here, they may turn around if they see Bill!" He ran for the corridor to follow Hickok. "Have the clerk take care of Trimble!"

He pounded down the corridor. Hickok was out the back door before he was halfway to it. Matt saw him raise his guns and begin firing, alternating them, the sound almost blending into one continuing explosion. Answering shots came from higher up.

He reached the door. As he did so, Hickok fired his last shot. He lowered his guns. A man was lying at the top of the open rear stairway. It was Teeters. Gridler was not in sight.

Hickok turned on him grimly. "Other one went back inside—I think I hit him." He was thumbing fresh cartridges into one gun. "I'll go up this way. You go back and up the front stairs. We've got him cornered."

Matt did so, but there was no more gun work to do. Gridler made it back to his room but he had dropped his gun before he got there. He was breathing out his last when they broke in on him.

Doc Adams got there a few minutes later, but by that time it was too late to do anything for Trimble, even. Before he died he told Hickok that he didn't know the men, that they weren't the ones he had seen in the stable back in Abilene.

"I shouldn't 'a' come," he whispered before the end. "I got . . . killed . . . for nothin' . . ."

Hickok looked at Matt. "He's right too," he said somberly. "I wonder . . ." he mused. "Teeters must have figured he was witness to that murder they did commit."

"The fools," Matt said; "they couldn't have been tried again for that one." He looked at Hickok. "If they'd held their fire, there wouldn't have been any grounds for arresting them."

You couldn't have enjoyed seeing them hang. We couldn't have 'just gone out and killed the pair of them'."

Hickok put his cold regard on Matt. "They downed Trimble," he said simply. "They had it coming." Then he seemed to forget it all. "I'd like to go somewhere and clean up," he said. "I could stand a good meal, and then I want to find a quiet game with a man-size limit and have some fun."

That was Hickok. Matt thought that if he didn't see the man again for a long time he could stand it. Three men had died, and all he could think of was food and cards. Teeters and Gridler and poor Trimble . . . they lay heavy on Matt Dillon's mind, and he hadn't fired a shot.

Printed in Great Britain
by Amazon

21258361R00092